# FORCE OF WILL

By

**Amy Booker**

eBook ISBN: 979-8-9906300-5-5

Published by Renaissan Publishing Limited, Cuyahoga Falls, Ohio

www.amybookerauthor.com

RENAISSAN
PUBLISHING
LIMITED

# Author's Note

If you've read my previous books, you'll know the chapter names are all song titles. Music has been an integral part of my life and always sets the mood for my writing. Whether it's the overall energy of a song, the lyrics, or even the title, that tone carries through into my written words on the page. The playlist and a link can be found at the back of each book, or you can find them on my website: www.amybooker-author.com.

# Dedication

For everyone who believes in second chances—

In love, in life, in the moments we thought were lost
but find their way back to us.

For the hearts that never stop beating for each other,
even when time and circumstance pull them apart.

For the songs that never fade, the rhythm that always
returns, and the love that was meant to last.

This is for you.

*"We are not the same persons this year as last; nor are those we love.*
*It is a happy chance if we, changing, continue to love a changed person."*

- W. Somerset Maugham

# The Sound of Winter

## WILL

**THE WHISKEY'S** packed despite this being a "secret" show. Another Angel hasn't played venues this small since their third album went gold, but breaking in a new drummer deserves intimacy – even if half of Blackmore Records' roster crashed the party. Twenty-eight years behind a kit and watching Lucas adjust the throne on my old DW still makes my hands twitch.

He catches my eye as he checks the tension on the kick pedal. The same pre-show ritual I taught him on his first junior kit. His hands are steady as he tests the hi-hat, muscle memory I recognize in my bones. The continuous glucose monitor sensor peeks out from under his sleeve as he reaches for the cymbal - another kind of ritual we've learned to live with, one I never had to think about during my own shows.

The band launches into their opener – one of the

tracks that made them famous, but already transformed by Lucas's touch. Where their old drummer
would have muscled through with showy fills, Lucas
lets the groove breathe. He's got my ear for dynamics
but his mother's instinct for space. When to push,
when to pull back.

The crowd surges forward as the chorus hits.
Industry types who've seen it all still can't help
moving when the hook lands. Lucas drives them there
with a build-up I taught him years ago, but he's added
his own flourishes. A subtle hi-hat pattern that wasn't
there in rehearsal. A way of opening up the crash
cymbal that makes the whole thing soar.

I find myself cataloging every choice, every variation. The way he's modified the bridge pattern to
better support their singer's tendency to rush. How
he's worked out a completely new groove for the pre-
chorus that somehow makes their old hit sound fresh.
All the little tricks I've taught him over the years, now
transformed into something entirely his own.

From my spot near the sound booth, I can see the
band's manager nodding along, phone forgotten in his
hand. Even the label reps look impressed, and those
guys wouldn't show excitement at the second coming.
Lucas has done what every musician dreams of – he's
made them forget they're working.

Our Sunday afternoon practice sessions flash
through my mind: Lucas banging on pots and pans at
five. At ten, graduating to his first real kit. At fifteen,

already better than half the pros I knew. Now, here he is, twenty-two, making one of LA's biggest bands sound better than they ever have. A far cry from the kid who used to sneak into my studio to practice when he should have been doing homework.

A subtle mistake in the pre-verse transition – something probably only I would catch – and I see his jaw tighten just like mine used to. But he recovers smoothly, turning the stumble into an intentional variation that works even better than the original pattern. That's all, Raine – she could always spin any mistake into gold. Some talents skip a generation. Some get perfectly blended into something new.

"He looks good up there."

The voice stops my heart quicker than any drum fill. Raine. I'd know that tone anywhere – the slight rasp that made her harmonies legendary, earned her spots on countless platinum records. A long way from the club singer I fell for years ago.

"Sounds good, too," I manage, not turning. Not yet. My fingers curl against my palm, an unconscious grip on phantom sticks. "Been practicing the new material for weeks."

"Like father, like son."

Now I turn. Mistake. She's standing closer than I expected, close enough that I catch the familiar scent of her perfume. Still the same after all these years. Her dark hair now has subtle silver streaks, but her hazel eyes are just as bright as the night she owned this stage.

"Maya here?" I ask, desperate for safe conversation.

"Running late. Client meeting." Pride colors her voice. "But she promised to catch the second set."

Lucas launches into the opening of Another Angel's new single – technically still under wraps, but the label's hoping this "leak" will build buzz. His kick drum pattern is precise but not mechanical, adding ghost notes where I wouldn't have thought to. Raine's eyes drift closed, swaying slightly. She always did feel rhythm in her bones.

"He's better than I was at his age."

"He had a good teacher."

The compliment lands heavy. We stand in loaded silence as Another Angel tears through their set. Every A&R rep and producer in the room is watching Lucas, evaluating, judging. This isn't just any band's new drummer – this is their shot at breaking through, and everyone knows it. But Raine watches him like only a mother can, that mix of pride and worry I remember from his first-grade school talent show.

The back of my neck prickles. Maya's arrived, hanging by the bar with that look she gets – too much like her mother's. Like she's reading every micro-expression, cataloging every almost-glance between us. Everything about her is like her mother, as if she's a carbon copy; same long brown hair, same soft features, same doe eyes, except Maya's are a warm brown. And they're always calculating.

"Heard you're doing backing vocals on their album," I say to Raine, just to break the tension.

"Mmm. Both albums, actually. Blackmore's keeping me busy."

Both albums. Right. Because Incendiary Ink is back in the studio next week. Because I'll be seeing her there, in that intimate space where we recorded our first album, where she was already my wife, already Maya's mom, already everything.

"Dad!" Lucas bounds off stage during the break, high on performance adrenaline. His dark blonde hair like mine wet with sweat. "Mom! You made it!"

He hugs Raine first — always did have a mama's boy streak. Maya slips through the crowd behind him, designer suit slightly rumpled from her rush to get here. When Lucas pulls back, she steals her own hug.

"Sorry I'm late, little brother. That merger meeting wouldn't end."

When Lucas hugs me, I catch Raine watching us, something soft in her expression. Maya hangs back, that knowing look in her eyes, again too much like her mother's for comfort.

"You killed it, kid," I tell him, meaning it. "That new bridge—"

"Changed up the pattern like you suggested." His grin could power Los Angeles. "Trent says it's defi-nitely making the album cut. Thanks for coming, all of you." He glances between us, too perceptive for his own good. "Means a lot."

"Wouldn't miss it," Raine says softly.

For a moment, we're just us – our little family, watching our son's dreams unfold. Then reality crashes back as the stage manager calls for Another Angel's second set.

"Knock 'em dead," I tell him.

"Make your old man proud," Raine adds.

Lucas practically bounces back to his kit, adjusting his monitors with practiced ease. I drift toward the bar, needing distance from the way Maya's watching us, her head tilted close to Raine's as they whisper together.

"He's really good, Will." Raine's voice follows me. "You did good with him."

"We did good," I correct, turning back. "Both of us."

She smiles – that genuine smile that still hits like a power chord – and returns to Maya. I lean against the bar, watching them together, trying to remember when our daughter got so grown up, so knowing. She's got her wedding coming up, but she can't help but meddle in the love lives of everyone around her. Always the romantic. Not sure where she got that from…

Thirteen years since Raine and I divorced. Ten since my second marriage imploded. Six months since her second marriage ended.

Not that I'm counting.

The music starts up again, Lucas's drums driving the band forward. He's got something I never had at his age – the patience to play exactly what the song needs, no showing off. His kick drum locks in with the bass line, solid as bedrock, while his cymbal work adds just enough color to make it interesting.

Maya catches my eye across the room, arching one eyebrow in a gesture so like her mother, it aches. Sometimes, I think our kids see right through us.

Lucas launches into another fill – this one entirely his own. His moment. His future. I lean against the bar, letting the familiar pulse of drums and bass wash over me, and try not to count how many beats until I'll get to talk to Raine again.

# Edge of Seventeen

## RAINE

**THE SECOND SET** kicks off with their latest single. I open my notebook, jotting down potential harmony points in the chorus – layered thirds in the hook, a descant line that could lift the bridge, subtle doubles to thicken the pre-chorus. The kind of polish that could take it from streaming hit to Grammy contender. Six other projects are due at Blackmore this week, but this one's personal.

My phone buzzes with another text from the showrunner at Netflix – third revision request this week. Apparently, the temp track I sent for their opening credits *"lacks emotional resonance."* Translation: someone's girlfriend in the production office thinks she's a vocal coach. Fine. I'll redo it tonight, layer in some ethereal clusters, and add that breathy pop texture they're all chasing lately. That, plus the Morrison backing tracks and that Target commercial that needs modulating up a half-step. Being every-one's go-to session vocalist means never having to worry about empty evenings.

"You should delegate more," Maya says, watching me type a quick response. "Isn't that why Blackmore gave you that corner office?"

"Vocal Production Supervisor looks good on paper." I slip the phone away. "But they still want my voice on everything."

Hard to complain. I've built this life carefully – the consistent studio work, the production credits, the reputation for delivering exactly what's needed, when it's needed. Years of saying yes to every session, every request, every chance to prove I could be both reliable and exceptional. Now, I'm the name producers drop when they want to impress new clients. The voice on a dozen diamond records. The final call on vocal arrangements for half the releases coming out of LA.

The irony doesn't escape me – becoming the expert on perfect arrangements while my personal life dissolved into chaos. Twice. First with the demands of Will's touring schedule, then with Eric's total disconnect from my world. At least the studio makes sense. Notes either work together or they don't. Harmonies either lift a song, or they fall flat. No gray areas, no messy emotions, no lawyers dividing up art collections and vacation homes.

My latest divorce barely made the industry gossip

channels. Just another brief in the LA Times: *"Vocal producer Raine Sheridan splits from entertainment attorney Eric Matthews."* Not like when Will and I ended – that was on the front page of Billboard, complete with speculation about Incendiary Ink's future and quotes from "sources close to the band." Amazing how twenty years can change your definition of scandal.

Maya leans against the bar beside me, a frown creasing her brow. "You're still working, though? At your son's show?"

I tuck the notebook away. "Force of habit."

"You know..." She takes a careful sip of her drink. "The wedding planner asked about music. Like, who's handling the reception performance."

Great. Another wedding detail I'm not ready to think about. "Maya, honey—"

"Relax. I told her we have plenty of time." She checks her phone. "Though speaking of time, how's the studio schedule looking next week? Dad mentioned—"

"Don't start."

She gives me that look – the same one she used to give the judge when she was interning at the courthouse. Like she's already ten steps ahead in an argument I don't even know we're having.

On stage, Lucas guides the band through a perfect build-up, his long blonde hair flying. He's adjusted his patterns since rehearsal last week when I stopped by with groceries – finally giving the vocalist room to breathe in the bridge. The kind of subtle adjustment that separates session players from stars. Every hit lands with intention, each ghost note purposeful.

"How's the new place?" Maya asks quietly.

"Getting there." Three months since I moved out of Eric's house. The new condo still feels like a hotel, but at least I don't wake up reaching for someone who isn't there anymore. "Lots of space for my home studio setup."

"You're still keeping the Neve console?"

"Your father's wedding gift?" I manage a small smile, though it aches. "Best piece of equipment I own. Set it up yesterday, actually. Between that and the new monitors..."

I let the sentence trail off. Eric never understood why I needed professional-grade equipment at home. Why I'd spend nights tweaking vocal arrangements instead of attending his firm's dinner parties where entertainment lawyers discussed music like it was just another asset to divide. Why music wasn't just a job I could leave at the studio. Maybe that's why it was easier to pack up my gear than my clothes – at least my equipment always made sense.

"I drove by the old house last week," Maya says carefully. "They're repainting."

"Good." I keep my voice neutral. "It needed updating."

"Mom..."

"I'm fine, honey. Really." I squeeze her hand. "The condo's closer to the studio anyway. And your brother's place. Speaking of which..."

"And the Morrison project?"

"Delivered yesterday. They want me back for overdubs next month." I'm good at this part – talking about work. Safer than discussing empty condos or failed marriages or how Will still stands exactly like he did twenty-four years ago, right down to the way he keeps time with his fingers against his leg when he's thinking.

He's by the sound booth now, studying Lucas with that laser focus that used to drive Incendiary Ink's producers crazy. Those piercing dark blue eyes of is narrowed with concentration. Nothing gets past him – not a single flubbed note or rushed fill.

"Room sounds good." His voice is suddenly closer. Right next to me. I surprisingly hadn't noticed him move towards us. "They've improved the monitors since our day."

Our day. When I sang backup on their first album. When we thought we could balance everything – tours, sessions, midnight recordings, little kids who needed more than musician parents could give.

"They've improved everything since our day." My smile stays professional. Studio polite. It's hard, but I manage. "But the room still has magic."

Maya's phone buzzes – probably her office. She

silences it without looking, watching the space between Will and me like she's calculating distances.

I should check my own messages. Should focus on Lucas. Should think about the Morrison vocals, the backing tracks for that new Netflix show, the commercial jingle due Thursday. Blackmore keeps me busy for a reason – I deliver, I'm reliable, I don't complicate things. I should be doing anything, but thinking about Will standing right next to me now.

How close he is. And how I still don't hate it.

Lucas guides the band through another new track – one I heard him practicing in their rehearsal space last week. He's completely restructured the groove, opening up space the original drummer never found. The vocalist finally hits that bridge cleanly, probably because he can actually hear himself. Lucas has pulled back the cymbal work, adjusted his dynamics. Musicians twice his age still haven't learned that sometimes the best thing you can do is get out of the way.

He's learned other lessons, too - I notice the quick sip of juice between songs, the practiced check of his monitor. Some rhythms become second nature, whether they're drum patterns or diabetes management. Though, I still catch myself watching, counting the minutes between checks like I did when he was first diagnosed.

The crowd's responding – even the A&R reps have stopped checking their phones. The band's manager is nodding along, probably already mentally revising their touring rates. Lucas has done what every musician dreams of – he's made them forget this is business.

I find myself marking mental notes: where to stack the harmonies, which phrases need doubling, how to lift the chorus without overwhelming the lead vocal. Things I'll need to know when we start tracking next week. The guitarist hits a slightly sharp note in the bridge, and I see Lucas adjust instantly, shifting the dynamics to cover it. That's all Will – that instinct for musical problem-solving mid-performance. Though the way he handles it, keeping everyone's confidence intact - that's a different kind of inheritance.

It's a long way from the teenager who used to sneak into my home studio, playing along to session tracks with headphones on, thinking I couldn't hear him through the walls. Who absorbed everything – Will's technical precision, my ear for arrangement, even Eric's business sense. Who called me in tears after his first failed audition, then spent six months woodshedding before trying again.

The other session players see it, too. That perfect blend of rock star energy and session player reliability. The same combination that kept me employed when my marriages fell apart, that built my reputation gig by gig, note by note. Lucas watched me rebuild myself twice through music.

The band launches into their closer. Lucas drives them home with a confidence that makes my chest tight. My baby boy, owning that stage like he was born to it.

I have three more sessions tomorrow. A call about Maya's wedding. A stack of contracts to review.

But right now, in this moment, I just listen to my son play.

The band hits their final chorus. Maya's hand finds mine, squeezing gently. Will's back by the sound board, but I feel his presence like a bassline – steady, constant, despite everything. Or, maybe *because* of everything.

Tomorrow, I'll be back in my office, juggling projects and deadlines. I'll review Maya's wedding arrangements, try to ignore the empty condo waiting at night, probably field another dozen requests for vocal arrangements that needed to be done yesterday.

But right now, watching Lucas own that stage, I remember why music grabbed me in the first place. Why I kept singing in clubs even while pregnant with Maya. Why I agreed to do backing vocals for an up-and-coming band called Incendiary Ink, even though I'd sworn off dating musicians. Why I built a career that let me stay in this world, even when it cost me everything else.

# Ghost of Days Gone By

WILL

"ONE MORE PASS ON THE BRIDGE."
Raphael's voice crackles through my headphones.
"Little rushed on the turnaround."

Twenty-five years we've been working together,
and he still catches every microsecond of imperfec-
tion. That's why he's got a million Grammys on his
shelf and a waiting list two years long. Though these
days, most of his clients are pop stars looking for
credibility, not aging rockers staging a comeback.

I adjust my throne, eyeing the constellation of
microphones surrounding my kit. Joe's been tweaking
their placement for three hours, chasing that elusive
perfect drum sound. Some things never change – even
with pro plugins and digital processing, getting the
right mix of room sound and close mics is still an art
form. Especially in Studio A, where the acoustics
have captured everything from our first album to last

year's Rock Hall tracks with Indigo King and Murderous Crows.

"Need anything shifted?" Joe ducks in, brandishing another drum mic. "That low tom's fighting me."

"Lower angle might help." I tap the rim. "It always did in the old days."

Joe grins. "Back when we had to get it right in one take?"

"Kids today don't know how good they have it." I return his smile. "Though some of us still prefer doing it right the first time."

"You good?" Chase catches my eye through the control room window. Translation: are you distracted because she'll be here next week?

I tap my snare twice. Good to go. Through the glass, I notice Mark staring at his guitar, fingers hovering over the strings without playing. He's been quiet all morning – more than usual, even for him. But before I can think too much about it, the click track counts in.

I sink into the groove. The bridge passage is tricky – lots of subtle dynamic shifts, ghost notes that need to float just behind the beat. Added complexity isn't usually my style, but Lucas's performance at the Whiskey last week got me thinking. Sometimes the best way to support a song is to get out of its way.

"That's the one." Raphael's approval fills my headphones. "Come listen."

Mark's already setting his guitar down when I enter the control room, his blue mohawk slightly wilted after six hours of tracking. His hands have a slight tremor I've never noticed before – probably from the marathon session.

"Killing it, old man," he manages, but the usual energy behind his teasing is flat. "Almost makes up for that disaster at rehearsal."

"Disaster?" I grab a bottle of water. "You mean when your amp caught fire?"

"Technical difficulties." He waves a hand, but doesn't meet my eyes. "Besides, Eliza got us all new gear after that."

Something's off in his tone. Mark's never cared about gear or label politics. Before I can probe deeper, Chase jumps in from the couch.

"Speaking of killing it, heard your kid murdered it at the Whiskey."

"Word travels fast." I try to keep my tone light, watching Mark drift toward the door.

"Everything travels fast when you're marrying the label president." Chase's grin widens. "Though I hear you weren't the only proud parent in attendance."

"Can we focus on the drums?" I gesture to the console where Joe and Raphael are making minute adjustments to EQ levels. The same console where we recorded our first album. Where Raine used to perch during playback, making notes about harmony placement while Maya slept in her carrier.

Mark's hand slips on his guitar case – another uncharacteristic fumble. Chase notices too, his expression shifting from teasing to concerned.

"Just saying." Chase holds up his hands in mock surrender, but his eyes follow Mark. "Some of us finally figured out what we wanted."

Right. Because Chase Avery, who spent twenty years pretending his relationship with Eliza Kerr was just casual fun, is now the expert on matters of the heart. Though watching him with Eliza's son lately, playing instant stepdad like he was born for it... maybe he's earned some wisdom.

"Complicated's different than confused." I keep my voice low, though Mark's already heading for the door, guitar forgotten. "And we're not having this conversation."

"Fine." Chase stretches, joints popping, but his eyes are on Mark's retreating back. "But you might want to figure it out before she gets here next week. Studio's smaller than the Whiskey."

The playback starts before I can respond. My drums fill the room, each hit precisely placed, every ghost note exactly where it should be. Different from our early records – more nuanced, more controlled. Back then, it was all power and flash, trying to prove something. Now, it's about serving the song. Growth, Raphael would call it. Or maybe just age.

"Nice work with the dynamics," Joe says,

tweaking a fader. "The way you're leaving space in the verses – really opens up room for—"

"The vocals," I finish. "Yeah."

Chase snorts softly behind me. So many years of friendship means he knows exactly where my mind went. To outro harmonies on our first album, to late-night recording sessions when Maya was still small enough to sleep between takes, to the way Raine used to watch me from the control room with that look that made me play better, made me want to be better.

"One more for the verses?" Raphael asks, professional as ever. He's watched enough band drama unfold in these rooms to write a book. Hell, he was here for our first album, watched Raine and me fall in love between takes. Watched us fall apart during the third album's sessions. "Then we can break for lunch."

Through the window, I catch Mark in the parking lot, just sitting in his car, head in his hands. Chase follows my gaze.

"Let's nail it." He picks up his bass to accompany me, covering Mark's missing guitar parts. "I've got a gear fitting at three. Apparently, being Rock and Roll Hall of Famers means we can't look like we buy our own equipment anymore."

"You mean your fiancée can't handle another amp explosion?" But the usual banter feels hollow with Mark's empty spot in the mix.

Back behind my kit, I try to focus on the click

track, on the way the overhead mics catch my cymbal work, on anything except the fact that in five days Raine will be standing in that iso booth, laying down the kind of harmony parts that turned our first album gold. Or the way Mark's hands shook on his strings, the silence where his riffs should be.

The verses flow easy – straight ahead groove, nothing fancy. Twenty-five years of muscle memory. My mind drifts to Lucas's showcase, to the way she marked notes in her book even while watching him play. Always working, always perfecting. Some things never change.

But some things do.

"Perfect," Raphael's voice breaks through my thoughts. "That's lunch. Back at two to tackle the outros?"

I start going over my kit, cataloging what needs adjusting for the afternoon session. Easier than thinking about next week, about small studios and scratch vocals and the way some harmonies never quite leave your head. Easier than wondering why our guitarist is sitting alone in his car instead of rehearsing.

"You know," Chase leans in the doorway, "some of us wasted a lot of years pretending we were fine with complicated."

"This is different." I focus on adjusting my kick pedal tension. "You and Eliza weren't married. Didn't have kids. Didn't get divorced and marry other people."

"No," he agrees. "We just spent twenty years scared of ruining what we had by admitting what we wanted. Real smart." He glances at his phone – probably another text from Eliza about wedding details or her son's band showcase. "Now I'm pushing fifty and learning how to be somebody's stepdad. Makes you think about what really matters."

His eyes drift to the parking lot, where Mark's car still sits.

"Chase."

"I'm just saying." He shrugs. "Life's short. And none of us are getting any better at hiding what we need."

I think about Maya's knowing looks at the Whiskey. About Lucas watching us both like he's solving a puzzle. About Mark's trembling hands on familiar strings. About the way my own hands still remember every rhythm of me and Raine.

"Let's just get the drums done," I say finally. "One track at a time."

Chase nods, knowing when to back off. "Whatever you say, drummer boy." He pauses at the door. "But you might want to work on your poker face before next week. It still fucking sucks. And we all know this studio has history."

And memories, I think, but don't say. Every booth, every corner haunted by late-night sessions and perfect takes, and the way her voice made everything soar. By all the things we try to hide until we can't anymore.

Joe pokes his head in. "Need help repositioning anything before we break?"

"Nah." I stand, stretching. "But maybe we should track the outros in Studio B next week. Better sound for vocals."

He gives me a look that says he's not buying it. "Studio B's booked. Some Netflix show needs their temp tracks redone."

Of course it is. Because that's exactly how this is going to play out.

# Going Under

RAINE

"LET'S run it again from the bridge." I mark another note in the margin of my chart. "Chase, try dropping to the third instead of staying on the fifth. Will, you've got the root."

Just another session. That's what I keep telling myself. I've done a thousand of these, built a career on being the voice that makes good tracks great. Professional. Reliable. Completely unfazed by working with my ex-husband and his best friend on their comeback album.

"Like old times," Chase grins through the control room window, his grey eyes sparkling. He looks better than he has in years – clear-eyed, steady. Amazing what love and sobriety can do. "Except you're on that side of the glass now."

"Some of us evolved." I adjust a fader, watching the meters dance. The pre-delay on Chase's vocal needs tweaking – just enough to let Will's harmony sit in its own space. "Speaking of evolution, try not to strain for that high harmony. It's not 1999 anymore."

Will's quiet laugh carries through the headphones. He's been watching me all morning with that steady drummer's focus, like he's trying to anticipate my next move.

"Ready?" Raphael asks from his spot behind the board. He's got that look he always gets when he knows he's capturing something special. "Take six."

The track starts, and I close my eyes, letting the familiar pieces fall into place. Chase's bass holding the foundation, Will's drums precise but fluid. Different from their early sound – more mature, more controlled. The kind of music that comes from knowing exactly who you are.

Their voices blend on the chorus just like they used to, Chase's raw edge and Will's steady tone. My part floats above, finding the spaces that need filling. Muscle memory. Like riding a bike, or falling in love, or—

*No. Professional thoughts only.*

"That's the one." Raphael's voice breaks through my concentration. "Raine? Thoughts?"

"Chase's pitch was better." I open my eyes, focusing on the console. "But Will, you rushed the pickup into the final chorus."

"Timing critique?" Will raises an eyebrow, but his smile is warm. "Times really have changed."

"Learned from the best." I keep my tone light, not letting those dark blue eyes get to me like they used to. "Again, from the chorus?"

"Actually," Raphael glances at the clock, "let's take a break. Joe's doing a coffee run."

"The usual?" Joe pokes his head in, notepad ready.

"God, yes." Twenty years and he still remembers – double shot vanilla latte, extra hot. "Thanks, Joe."

"Black for me," Will adds. "And—"

"Green tea, I know." Joe rolls his eyes. "Chase's new health kick is the talk of the studio."

"Hey, I'm trying here." Chase stretches. "Eliza's got me eating kale."

I busy myself with the console while they place orders, tweaking effects settings that don't need tweaking. Easier than watching Will in the iso booth, the same booth where he used to watch me record harmonies for their first album. Where he'd tap rhythms on his leg while I worked out vocal arrangements, his pride so obvious it made me sing better.

"Lucas mentioned you're helping with his home studio setup," Will says through the talkback.

Safe territory. Our son. Our shared pride. "Just some basic guidance. Though he's got good instincts."

"Gets that from you." Will adjusts his headphones over his shaggy blonde hair. "The technical ear."

"Pretty sure the obsession with equipment is all you." I think of Lucas's detailed questions about preamps and compression settings. "He called yesterday asking about vintage mic preamps versus modern ones."

"Did you tell him about that ancient preamp you used to swear by?" Will asks.

"The one you insisted on finding for the first album?" I can't help smiling at the memory. "Three different studios, and you wouldn't let us record my parts until—"

"Got it!" Joe's back, balancing a drink carrier. "One green tea for the reformed rock star, black coffee for the timekeeper, and one unnecessarily complicated latte for the vocal queen."

"You're a saint." I take my cup, grateful for the interruption.

"Speaking of complicated," Raphael says, accepting his americano, "these harmony arrangements are something else, Raine. Different from what you usually do for other artists."

"Well, I know their voices." I take a careful sip. "Twenty-five years of context helps."

"Plus, she can't help showing off a little." Chase's eyes dance over his tea. "Now that she's the big shot producer."

"Says the man engaged to the label president."

"Touché." He grins. "Though some things don't change. Will still air-drums during vocal takes."

"I do not—" Will starts.

"You absolutely do," Raphael and I say together.

The studio fills with easy laughter, and for a moment it feels just like it used to. Before farewell tours and rehab stays and divorce papers. Before second marriages and empty houses and grown children planning their own lives.

"These harmonies remind me of that ballad on the second album," Raphael says, ever the professional. "The one about—"

"Don't," Chase interrupts softly, and I could kiss him for it. Some songs we don't need to revisit.

I check the clock. "We should get back to it. I want to try a different approach on the bridge, maybe layer the harmonies instead of stacking them."

"Whatever you think." Will's voice is careful, neutral. "You're the expert."

"Hardly." I pull up the track again. "Just been doing this a while."

"Long enough to know what works." Chase settles his headphones back in place over his short, dark hair. "And what doesn't."

The double meaning hangs in the air, but he doesn't push it. Maybe sobriety really has made him more subtle.

"From the bridge then?" I ask, already reaching for the faders.

Professional. Reliable. Just another session.

*If I repeat it enough times, maybe I'll believe it.*

# Your Touch

## WILL

"YOU'RE DISTRACTED." Maya looks up from her pad thai. "Studio session go okay?"

I've been pushing noodles around my plate for ten minutes, thinking about the way Raine's voice wrapped around the harmonies today. About how natural it felt, having her back in the control room. Our Thursday dinner ritual at Lotus Thai usually helps clear my head, but tonight even the familiar comfort of Maya's company isn't enough.

"Dad?"

"Sorry." I focus on my daughter's too-perceptive expression. "Session was fine. Your mom's still the best in the business."

"I know." She stirs her tea, too casual. "That's why I asked her to sing at the wedding."

The words hit like a missed cue.

"She's doing *At Last*."

My chopsticks freeze halfway to my mouth. *Our wedding song.* The one she used to sing at clubs, the one playing when I first saw her on stage. The one she surprised me with at our wedding reception.

"Dad?"

"Good choice." My voice sounds steady. Almost natural. "Classic."

"It was your song, right?" As if she doesn't know. As if she hasn't seen the wedding video a hundred times.

"Maya Elizabeth."

"What?" Pure innocence. "I just thought it would be nice. Mom already agreed."

Of course, she did. Which means she spent all day in the studio, directing my harmonies, critiquing my timing, and never said a word about planning to sing our wedding song at our daughter's reception.

"When did you ask her?"

"Last week." Maya sips her tea. "After Lucas's show."

The Whiskey. When she was watching us watch each other. Planning this all along.

Though lately, everything feels like a plan. Like Raine choosing a condo three blocks from my house after her divorce, when she could have bought anywhere in LA. Like Maya suggesting we keep our standing Thursday dinner at this Thai place, which just happens to be halfway between my place and Raine's new building. Even the route home takes me past her street – not that I'm counting the steps from her front door to mine.

Four hundred and twelve. Give or take.

"You're as subtle as a crash cymbal, you know that?"

"I have no idea what you're talking about." But her smile is pure Raine – that hint of mischief she used to get before surprising me with late-night studio visits. "Besides, we need to talk about the ceremony music, too."

"One ambush at a time, please."

She laughs – her mother's laugh. "Come on, dad. You really think Mom suggested *At Last*?"

"She didn't?"

"She tried to talk me out of it. Said it might be too complicated."

The server clears our plates. I try to push away the memory of Raine in that ivory dress, focus on my daughter instead of wondering if her mother was thinking about that moment today in the studio.

"How's the rest of the planning going?" Safe territory. "Devon's family still flying in from Boston?"

"For the menu tasting next month." She pulls out her phone. "His mom's got strong opinions about the cake. Though not as strong as Devon's opinions about the band."

I smile despite myself. Devon's a good kid – corporate lawyer who quotes Zeppelin lyrics in legal briefs and geeks out over vintage guitars. The kind of son-in-law a musician couldn't help but like.

"He's still pushing for the string quartet to learn 'Stairway'?"

"Actually, he had another idea." She scrolls through her notes. "About the processional..."

"Maya."

"The planner needs to know about dietary restrictions first," she continues smoothly. "Chase mentioned you're all doing that clean eating thing for the tour?"

"His idea. Something about maintaining sobriety through healthy choices." I shake my head. "Never thought I'd see Chase Avery drinking green smoothies."

"People change." She gives me a pointed look. "Grow up. Figure out what they want."

"Maya."

"I'm just saying." She scrolls through what's clearly a prepared list. "Like how mom chose this neighborhood for her fresh start. Right by that little coffee shop you both love. The one with the jazz brunch on Sundays?"

And there it is. The real reason for tonight's dinner. Maya's never been able to resist building a case, presenting her evidence piece by piece.

"I ran into her there last weekend," she continues innocently. "She said the croissants remind her of that place in Paris. You know, from your honeymoon?"

"The wedding song was enough for one night, counselor."

She finally puts the phone down. "I just think it's interesting…."

"Here we go…" *Interesting*, never means *interesting*.

"How you both ended up here. How you light up when you talk about music. How you still finish each other's sentences in the studio."

I signal for the check. "You're reading too much into things."

"Maybe." She catches my hand across the table. "Or maybe I just pay attention. Like how you both take the long way home just to go past each other's streets."

The check arrives before I can respond. Maya grabs it before I can protest.

"My treat," she says. "Consider it a thank you for not freaking out about the wedding song."

"I'm not freaking out."

"No," she agrees. "You're just thinking about how beautiful Mom's going to sound singing it."

Sometimes I forget she's not that little girl who used to sit in my lap during soundcheck anymore. That she's grown into this perceptive woman who sees right through both her parents.

"The song will be beautiful," I say finally. "Your mom never does anything halfway."

"I know." She stands, kissing my cheek. "That's what I'm counting on."

Outside, the LA night is cool for once. Maya hugs me tight, and for a moment she's small again, falling asleep in the studio while her mother laid down vocal tracks.

"Love you, Dad. See you next Thursday?"

"Same time, same place." I watch her head for her car. "Even when you're being impossible."

"Must be hereditary." She grins over her shoulder. "Try not to think about Mom's condo being on your way home."

I stand there until her taillights disappear, thinking about tomorrow's session. About wedding songs and lawyers who never really stop cross-examining their parents. About how some choices echo longer than others, like someone moving to a neighborhood where every street holds the possibility of running into your ex at your favorite coffee shop.

And how sometimes your daughter sees the truth you're trying not to admit to yourself.

My car's pointing toward home, but I find myself taking the long way. *Just to check the street lighting*, I tell myself. Just to make sure the security guard's at his post. The neighborhood's safe – it's why I chose it, why I suggested it when she mentioned wanting a fresh start after Eric – but it can't hurt to drive by. Make sure she's settling in okay.

Her windows are dark. Of course they are – she's

probably still at the studio, laying down vocals for that Netflix show. But there's a soft glow from what I think is her home studio on the second floor. The one she set up right after moving in, where Lucas practices sometimes. Where she's probably working out arrangements for our daughter's wedding. For our song.

*Jesus. My fucking imagination sure runs wild, doesn't it?*

I grip the wheel tighter, forcing myself to drive past. Tomorrow, we'll be back in the studio, keeping things professional. Tonight, I'm just a concerned friend. A neighbor checking on new security measures.

Nothing more.

Even if I don't quite believe it myself.

# Drumming Song

## RAINE

**THE PHOTO ALBUM** is heavier than I remember. Years of dust, maybe. Or just the weight of memories I've been avoiding. Maya sits at my kitchen island, still in her court clothes, having just lugged over Devon's ancient VCR after a full day of depositions.

"I can't believe he still has this thing," Maya says, untangling cords. "Though apparently, it's worth something now."

"Devon's getting as bad as your father about vintage equipment."

The kitchen's still half-organized, weeks after moving in. Empty cabinets waiting to be filled, except for my coffee station - the only thing I've properly unpacked besides my studio equipment. The open floor plan and modern fixtures are everything Eric's formal mansion wasn't. That was the point.

"Here." I pull out the leather-bound album, grateful for the distraction from replaying today's studio session in my mind. Will's careful distance, the way he kept time with his fingers when he thought I wasn't looking. So different from his easy manner earlier this week. "Your father hired the best photographer we could afford back then. Which meant Chase's cousin with a decent camera."

"Before you were all rockstars?" Maya opens to the ceremony photos. "Oh wow, dad looks so young."

He does. Standing at the altar in his black tux, trying to hide how nervous he was. His shaggy hair tamed somewhat for once. His smile shaky. This was before the platinum records, before the world tours. When Incendiary Ink was still playing clubs and I was doing session work between club gigs.

"Found it." Maya holds up a photo from the reception. "When you surprised him with *At Last.*'"

I don't need to look. That image is burned into my memory – grabbing the mic in my wedding dress, Chase and Mark backing me up on borrowed instruments. Will's face when he recognized the opening chords. Back when we thought love could conquer anything, even tour schedules and midnight recording sessions.

"Dad never could hide his feelings when you sang." Maya turns another page. "Speaking of which... he knows about you singing that song."

"You told him?"

"Last night. At dinner." She watches my face carefully. "He said it was a good choice. That you'll make it beautiful."

Of course, he did. Always the gentleman, even when I'm ambushing him with our wedding song at our daughter's reception.

"Oh my god," Maya laughs suddenly. "Look at Chase giving his best man speech. What was he even wearing?"

"That was actually tame for Chase back then." I study the photo - Chase in his slightly rumpled blue ruffled tux, Eliza in the background looking elegant as always in a designer suit. Even then, everyone could see what they refused to admit for years.

"You ready for dress shopping tomorrow?" Maya asks, smoothly changing the subject. "Devon's mom flies in next weekend to see the Plaza Hotel space, so we need to at least narrow down styles before she arrives with her opinions."

"The Plaza." I shake my head. "Quite a step up from the little chapel where your father and I—"

Through the window, a familiar car glides past. Right on schedule.

"He worries," Maya says softly.

"What?"

"Dad. Ever since Eric..." She nods toward the window. "Every night, like clockwork. Pretending he's just checking the neighborhood."

I move to busy myself with the VCR cables. "The neighborhood's perfectly safe. It's why I chose it."

"Right. The neighborhood." Maya's tone is pointed. "Nothing to do with being three blocks from Dad's place."

"The real estate agent suggested—"

"Speaking of Dad," she interrupts, pulling out her phone. "Devon's going shopping with Dad tomorrow. Apparently, there's some vintage Gretsch he's thinking about adding to his collection."

"I'm sure your father will love that." I try not to think about how Will's face lit up today when I mentioned Devon's guitar obsession. How for a moment it felt like old times in the studio, before he retreated back into careful professionalism. "He's always saying Devon's the son-in-law he deserved, given his own equipment addiction."

"They can enable each other while we find my dress tomorrow." Maya scrolls through her calendar. "Unless you need to work on those Netflix tracks..."

"No, I finished the final mix today. Between takes with your father pretending everything was completely normal."

The words slip out before I can stop them.

Maya sets down her phone. "How bad was it?"

"Professional." I reach for the wedding video, needing something to do with my hands. The case is worn, the label faded. "Will's very good at being professional."

"Mom."

"The tracks came out fine. Chase made some joke about my producing style getting militant. Your father just nodded and counted in the next take."

The video feels heavier in my hands. Will used to play it every anniversary, back when we still believed in those. I wonder if he'll watch it before the wedding, before he has to hear me sing that song again.

"Devon thinks it's romantic," Maya says quietly. "The way you both still..."

"Maya."

"What? I'm just saying. He's a corporate lawyer who collects guitars and reads Billboard charts. He notices things." She taps the photo album. "Like how dad's vintage guitar collection started the same year you left. Or how you're producing your best vocals after Eric."

"You're as bad as your father with the timing comments." I slide the tape into the VCR. "Always analyzing every beat."

"Must be the lawyer in me." She fiddles with the tracking. "Though Devon's the one who pointed out you chose this place the day after Dad mentioned his favorite coffee shop moved to this neighborhood."

The screen flickers to life. Younger versions of Will and me, believing in forever. The ceremony plays silently while Maya adjusts the volume.

"Got it!" Sound crackles through. Chase's best

man speech, full of inside jokes about drum solos and vocal warmups. Will in the background, watching me in that way he still sometimes does in the studio when he thinks I'm focused on the console.

Like today, between takes, before he pulled back into himself.

"There's the surprise," Maya says softly as the first notes of "*At Last*" fill the room. My voice, younger but still sure, backed by the band who would become family. Will's face as he realized what was happening.

I push up from the couch. "I should prep for tomorrow—"

"Mom." Maya pauses the video. "You can't avoid the dress shopping. The fitting room is already booked."

"I meant the Netflix deadline for Monday."

"Right. Because you definitely need to work on tracks you just told me you finished." She follows me into the kitchen. "Instead of dealing with the fact that you're both pretending this neighborhood thing is a coincidence."

Through the window, Will's car makes another pass. Definitely not helping my case.

"He's not the only one who worries," Maya says quietly.

"I'm fine." I start gathering the photos. "The dress shopping will be fine. The wedding will be fine."

"And Dad?"

I think about today's session. The careful space he kept between us, so different from our easy rhythm earlier this week. How neither of us mentioned the wedding song he apparently knows about, or this neighborhood, or the fact that we're running out of excuses for the choices we keep making.

"You know what Devon said?" Maya gathers her things. "He was going through the contracts for Plaza's house band. Said it was funny how they already had the sheet music for *'At Last.'*"

"Maya."

"Just an observation. He is a lawyer, after all." She kisses my cheek. "Pick you up at ten tomorrow?"

I walk her to the door, where she pauses. "One more thing. I love you, Mom. I just want to see you happy."

Nodding at her, I whisper, "I know." The emotions had welled up in my throat, and I couldn't bring myself say anything else.

I stand in the doorway until her car disappears, then climb the stairs to my studio. The Neve preamp Will gave me sits ready, though there's nothing left to mix tonight. No more tracks to polish, no more harmonies to perfect.

Just the quiet, and the knowledge that tomorrow I'll help our daughter try on wedding dresses while trying not to think about the way Will watched me in the studio today. The way he still watches me, when he thinks I don't notice.

Through the window, I hear his car one last time. Making sure everything's secure.

To be honest, I'm not sure that I am. Not as my heart skips a beat just thinking about him.

# So Far Away

## WILL

"YOUR KICK DRUM'S DRAGGING." I steal a french fry from Lucas's plate. "Third verse of the new single."

"My kick drum's perfect." Lucas guards the rest of his fries. "And you're deflecting."

"He's definitely deflecting." Mark signals our server for another round, his blue mohawk catching the light from Salvatore's pendant lamps. "Been doing it all weekend."

Salvatore's on Sunday nights. Our tradition since Lucas started playing seriously, though lately, Mark joins more often than not. Something about the worn leather booths and the steady stream of classic rock from the speakers makes shop talk flow easier. Makes everything flow easier, really.

"I'm not—"

"Then ask me about the dress shopping." Lucas grins. "You know you want to."

I concentrate on my burger instead. Sunday dinner with my son is supposed to be safe territory. Even with Mark joining us - which he usually does - the conversation typically sticks to music and touring. Not wedding details. Not dress fittings. Not—

"Uh oh." Lucas's voice drops. "Three tables back. By the bar."

I don't need to turn. "Becca's here?"

"New haircut," Mark says after a casual glance. "New guy looks like he works in finance."

"You want to move tables?" Lucas asks.

"Why?" I genuinely want to know. "Your fries are getting cold."

Mark shakes his head, amused. "Man, I forgot how much you don't care."

"Not caring implies effort." I steal another fry. "I just... don't think about her at all."

Through the front windows, I watch her leave with her date, sliding into his BMW. Probably another investment banker. Thirteen months. That's all it took to realize you can't fix loneliness with stability. Becca wanted the rockstar who played charity events with her firm, who'd settle into corporate parties and country club memberships. Instead, she got a drummer who still wrote rhythm patterns in his sleep, who couldn't stop comparing her charity galas to the clubs where Raine used to sing.

The divorce was as efficient as our courtship. Clean division of assets, no messy emotions. No kids to consider, no shared history to untangle. She kept the country club membership. I kept my drums. Neither of us looked back.

"You know what your problem was with Becca?" Mark sets down his beer. "You thought normal meant happy."

"My problem with Becca was thinking I was ready to move on." The words slip out before I can stop them.

Lucas and Mark exchange glances. *Again.*

"Friday was fine." I focus on my plate, changing the subject. "We got the tracks done."

"Yeah, super fine." Mark leans back, pushing his empty plate away. "That's why you and Raine barely spoke between takes. That's why Chase kept giving me those looks."

"Chase always gives looks." But Lucas is watching me now, too. *Great.* "The album's coming together. That's what matters."

"Sure." Mark sets down his drink. "Though usually, you two can't shut up about harmony arrangements and mic placement. Friday, you practically hid behind your kit."

"Need another round?" Our server appears at Lucas's elbow.

Lucas glances at my expression, then at his

continuous glucose monitor. "Water for me. Early session tomorrow."

"Let the kid live a little," Mark says, ordering another beer for himself.

But Lucas just shrugs - some routines are non-negotiable, even if Uncle Mark wants to let it slide once in a while.

"Mom seemed quiet yesterday, too," Lucas says carefully. "At the dress shop."

My hand tightens on my glass. "Lucas."

"What? Just making conversation." He has that same innocent tone Maya gets when she's building a case. "Though she did mention the studio's booked all week..."

"Another Angel tracking vocals?" Mark asks.

"Another Netflix show." I try to keep my voice neutral. "Some theme song thing."

Tomorrow's schedule sits heavy in my pocket. Three tracks to polish, then Raine's coming in to work on the theme sequence. Some streaming show about time travel and second chances - the universe's idea of a joke, probably. She'll be in Studio B all week, her voice filling the same space where we recorded all our albums. Where she used to bring baby Maya during late-night sessions.

Chase sent the rough cuts over this morning. Said the label wants something "nostalgic but contemporary." Said Raine's got some ideas about layered harmonies and vocal effects. Said a lot of things that weren't "by the way, she's singing your wedding song at Maya's reception."

"The Netflix thing's a big deal," Lucas offers. "Mom's excited about the creative control they're giving her."

"Yeah?" I try to sound casual. "She mention what she's planning?"

"Just that she's drawing inspiration from some older arrangements." His tone is too innocent. "Songs that meant something to people."

"Speaking of your mom," Mark takes a swig of his beer, settling in. "Did she really move into your neighborhood? Chase mentioned—"

"Since when do you and Chase gossip?"

"Since you two started acting weird in the studio." He shrugs. "Twenty-five years of friendship, man. We notice things."

"Devon's coming by the studio next week," Lucas says, clearly trying to change the subject. "Wants your opinion on some vintage Gretsch he and Dad bought yesterday."

"Smart kid." Mark nods approvingly. "Getting the father-in-law on his side with equipment talk."

"Devon's alright." More than alright, actually. The kind of son-in-law who gets both the music and the business side. Who makes my daughter happy. Who apparently helps pick out wedding songs that—

"Dad?" Lucas is watching me too carefully. "You okay?"

"Fine." I reach for my wallet. "Just thinking about tomorrow's session."

"Right. Tomorrow's session." Mark exchanges another look with Lucas. "When you'll totally act normal about whatever happened Friday."

"Nothing happened Friday."

"Sure." Lucas starts gathering his things. "That's why Mom spent half of yesterday not talking about you."

The check arrives before I can respond. I grab it quickly - Sunday dinners are always on me, even if Lucas is making his own money now. Even if he's about to go on tour himself, playing bigger venues than I did at his age.

"Speaking of the tour," Mark says as we head out. "Which we weren't. You talk to your mom about the schedule? Both bands being on the road at the same time..."

"She's fine with it." Lucas holds the door. "Said she did enough worrying about touring musicians for one lifetime."

"Madison Square Garden, though." Mark grins. "Opening week. Not bad for your first major tour."

Pride mixes with something else in my chest. Took us three albums to book MSG. Another Angel's doing it almost right out of the gate. Even though they've been around for a while, they always seem to be right at the edge of making it big. Maybe now they will.

"The schedule's brutal," Lucas admits, checking his phone. "A long three months. But the management team's solid. Everything planned down to the minute." Including the things he doesn't mention - the medical staff vetted, emergency contacts in every city, backup supplies arranged. Some concerns you learn to handle without discussing.

"Better than our first tour." I try to keep my tone light. "Playing every dive bar between here and Detroit. Living on gas station coffee and promises."

"Now they've got personal chefs and massage therapists." Mark shakes his head. "These kids today don't know how good they have it."

Lucas pockets his phone. "The label's talking about Asia after Europe. If the single performs."

*If.* Like there's any doubt. The song's already climbing the streaming charts, and that's before the push they're planning. Before the video drops. Before Lucas's drumming gets the attention it deserves.

"You know," Mark says carefully, "some of us remember what you were like during that second marriage. With Becca."

"Mark." I'm getting whiplash from his topic changes. But then, Mark's never been one to walk a straight line with his conversations. He just says whatever pops into his head at the time.

"Just saying. There's a difference between moving on and running away." He claps my shoulder. "See you tomorrow, drummer boy. Try to actually speak to your ex-wife between takes."

I watch them leave - Mark's mohawk visible even in the dim lot, Lucas already on his phone probably texting Maya about our dinner. About how their father still can't handle conversations about wedding planning or dress shopping or songs that remind him of what he lost.

Tomorrow we'll be back in the studio. Tomorrow I'll have to still pretend I don't know about '*At Last*,' about Maya's plans, about the way Raine's voice still hits me harder than any drum fill.

I check my phone. Three texts from Maya about Devon's guitar questions. One from Chase about tomorrow's session. Nothing from Raine.

Not that I'm counting.

# 23

~~~

RAINE

ERIC'S SHIRT must have gotten mixed in with my things during the move. One last Brooks Brothers button-down, still smelling like his cologne - something expensive and subtle that probably has notes of cedar and success. I add it to the donation pile. Amazing how life together can be sorted into such neat boxes: keep, donate, forget.

Three weeks in the new place and I'm finally tackling these unopened cartons. Though technically the studio was priority, so it wasn't procrastination. At least, that's what I keep telling myself.

Something small and fuzzy catches my attention at the bottom of the next box. I know what it is before I pull it out - a slightly squashed pink elephant, missing one googly eye. Will's triumphant prize from the ring toss at Santa Monica Pier, back when we were too young to care that carnival games were rigged.

"Had to win you something," he'd said, so serious about it. "First real date and all."

A car door closes outside. Familiar engine idle. I wait for the sound of him driving away - his usual evening check that everything's secure. Instead, footsteps on my front walk.

The doorbell catches me off guard.

Will stands on my front step holding a coffee creamer. French vanilla, the expensive kind I always use.

"Wasn't sure if you were settled yet." He shifts the bag between hands nervously. "Grocery shopping."

*At ten at night. Right.*

"Thanks." I take the creamer, trying to ignore how this domestic gesture feels more intimate than a studio session. "Want to come in?"

"I should..." He glances past me at the boxes scattered across my living room. At the small pink elephant still in my hand. "Oh."

I resist the urge to hide it behind my back like a teenager caught with contraband. "Just unpacking."

"Right." His eyes linger on the elephant. "I can't believe you kept that."

"Well, you did win it fair and square." Even though we both knew the carnival worker took pity on his terrible aim. "Want some coffee? Since you're out grocery shopping so late and all."

The ghost of a smile. But I think I see a bit of hesitance in his eyes. "I should go. Early session tomorrow."

"Right." I step back, giving him space. "Thanks for the creamer."

He nods, already turning away. Then stops. Eyeing me carefully. "You okay here? By yourself?"

The question hangs between us. *Am I okay here?* The concern in his voice is so different from Eric's efficient emails about property division and forwarded mail. My ex-husband hasn't even asked where I moved to, much less driven by nightly to check the security.

"I'm good." I gesture vaguely at the boxes. "Just attempting to get somewhat organized."

His eyes catch on Eric's shirt in the donation pile. Something flickers across his face, but he just nods. He shifts his weight, half-turned to leave but not quite going. The same way he hovers by the console in the studio, like he's always fighting the urge to step closer.

"Lucas said the dress shopping went well."

"It did." I shift the creamer to my other hand, needing something to do. "Maya's got your eye for detail."

"And your ability to run a room." That small smile again. "Apparently, she had the whole boutique jumping."

The conversation feels safer with Maya between

us. Almost normal, if you ignore the way he's still standing half-turned to leave, like he doesn't trust himself to fully face me. Like he's too aware of being in my space rather than the neutral ground of the studio.

He's halfway down the walk when he turns back. "That elephant..."

"Yeah?"

"I practiced that ring toss for an hour before you got to the pier." He shoves his hands in his pockets. "Spent my last forty bucks trying to get good enough to impress you."

Before I can respond, he's gone. The familiar sound of his car starting up, pulling away. Not that he won't drive by again later, checking the street lights, making sure everything's secure.

Eric hasn't asked once if I feel safe here. Hasn't wondered about my new neighborhood or living situation. His assistant sent the emails, his lawyer handled the paperwork. Clean. Professional. The way he handled everything.

I stand at the window long after his car disappears. Something settles in a box behind me, and I nearly jump out of my skin I was so lost in thought. Forty-eight, successful, and jumping at night sounds in my own home.

*I'm fine. Yes, I'm alone for the first time ever, but I'm totally fine.*

The silence feels different here. In Eric's house,

quiet meant distance - separate wings, separate lives. With Will, even after the divorce, silence was never really empty. There were always kids practicing instruments, band rehearsals, family dinners. Even when we lived apart, our lives stayed tangled through Maya and Lucas, through music, through the easy rhythm we found as co-parents.

This is different. Maya's planning her wedding, Lucas is about to tour. For the first time in my life, I'm truly alone. No husband, no kids at home, no timeline for when that changes. Just me and these boxes and the endless possibility that this is what the rest of my life looks like.

Funny how being alone feels different at forty-eight than it did at twenty-five. Back then, solitude meant freedom. Now it comes with 3 AM thoughts about growing old by myself, about empty holiday tables, about who to call when the power goes out or the pipes burst.

*Except.*

Except Will brought me coffee creamer at ten PM just to check on me. Except he drives by every night like clockwork, making sure I'm safe. Except I chose this neighborhood, this street, this view of his evening route.

My phone buzzes - Maya sending dress alteration details. Such a simple text, but it launches an avalanche of questions. Who'll help me shop for a mother-of-the-bride dress? Who'll zip me up, tell me if it's too much or not enough? Eric's probably already RSVP'd with his new girlfriend. Will's going to be there, looking devastatingly handsome in whatever suit Maya picks out, or – actually, probably a tux, watching me sing our song...

I press my forehead against the cool window glass. Outside, the street is quiet. For now. Until he drives by again, pretending he just happened to take the long way home. Until I pretend I'm not waiting to hear his engine.

I add another of Eric's shirts to the donation bag, but the pink elephant goes on a shelf in my studio. Next to the Neve preamp Will gave me, the one Eric always said was taking up too much space in our house. Some things you keep, some you give away. And some you hold onto even when you're pretending not to remember why they mattered in the first place.

I set his creamer in my perfectly organized kitchen, right next to the coffee station. Pretending I don't understand exactly what it means that he noticed my favorite creamer was missing from the studio's kitchen last week. That he remembered the brand, the flavor, the way I can't start a session without it. That he's still keeping track of my little details while Eric probably couldn't name my coffee order if his next case depended on it.

The street is quiet now, but it won't stay that way.

He'll be back, just like he has been every night since I moved in. Making sure everything's secure. Making sure I'm okay.

Making it impossible to pretend I don't know exactly why I chose this neighborhood.

# Through Glass

## WILL

**THE STUDIO FEELS** different at seven AM. Quieter. Like the sound-proofed walls hold secrets instead of music. I'm adjusting mic stands around my kit when I hear the front door open, followed by familiar footsteps in the hallway.

Of course, she's early, too.

"Oh." Raine stops in the doorway. "I didn't... I thought I'd be first."

She's wearing the same sweater from last night, when she stood in her doorway holding that pink elephant. Not that I'm thinking about that. About her alone in that big empty condo, sorting through boxes of memories.

"Just setting up." I focus on the kick drum mic. "Chase texted that he'll be late."

"When isn't he?" She sets her bag down, closer to my kit than necessary. The scent of vanilla hits me -

she's already been to the coffee shop. Or, she used the creamer I brought her. Not that I'm thinking about that, either. "The overhead's crooked."

I glance up. "What?"

"The mic." She points. "It's not catching the full kit spread."

Before I can stop her, she's beside me, reaching past to adjust the stand. Her sleeve brushes my arm. Neither of us moves.

"Better?" Her voice is soft, professional. But she hasn't stepped back.

I test the kick pedal, hyper-aware of her presence. "Yeah."

"Good." Still not moving. "About last night—"

"You don't have to—"

"I just meant—"

We both stop. Twenty-five years of making music together, and we can't string a sentence between us.

"The creamer," she finally manages. "It was thoughtful."

"Just being neighborly." The lie tastes bitter. Like we don't both know I drive by her place every night. Like she hasn't noticed me checking her street, her condo, her security.

She finally steps back, but not far. "Right. Neighborly."

*Is that disappointment in her voice?*

The morning sun slants through the high windows, catching the silver in her hair. She's fidgeting with her phone like she needs something to do with her hands, like she doesn't feel this thick air between us, this weight of everything we're not saying.

"Maya sent the alterations schedule," she says finally.

"Yeah." I adjust a cymbal that doesn't need adjusting. "Lucas mentioned the dress shopping went well."

"It did. She's..." Raine trails off, and I know she's thinking the same thing I am. Our little girl, planning her wedding. While we stand here pretending we're just old friends. Just neighbors. Just exes.

"Raine—"

She takes a step closer, and suddenly, there's no air in the room. She's close enough I can see the flecks of green in her hazel eyes, the way her pulse jumps at her throat. The scent of her perfume overwhelms me, and I step even closer, my fingers instinctively reaching up to tuck her hair behind her ear. Just that quick touch shoots through me like lightning.

Her eyes close slowly, and she leans toward me, just as I'm leaning towards her. Every inch of me flickers and flutters with anticipation, with memories, with history, with want. Just the thought of kissing her, again, after all this time, fills me with a feeling of everything being so right that it scares the shit out of me.

She tilts her head up, and I bend mine closer, our

warm breath mingling between us. An inch more from either of us will change everything. We're so close to the edge of a cliff I think we've been destined for.

Close enough to—

The front door slams. Chase's voice echoes down the hall, followed by Mark's laugh.

Raine practically jumps away, already heading for the control room. By the time the others arrive, she's safely behind the glass, all business. Professional distance restored.

But I notice her hands shaking slightly as she reaches for a knob on the sound board.

And I've completely forgotten what I was going to play.

*Fuck me.*

"Morning, children!" Chase breezes in, green smoothie in hand. "Everyone survive the weekend?"

I focus on my kit, not looking through the control room window where I know Raine's doing the same thing I am - trying to steady her breathing, trying to look normal.

"Will's early," Mark observes, setting up his guitar. "That's suspicious."

"Had to check the drum mics," I manage. Like I haven't been here since six-thirty, killing time until I heard her car pull up. Like I haven't been thinking about last night since I left her driveway.

Through the glass, I watch Raphael walk in and

settle beside Raine at the console. She's nodding at something he's saying, completely professional. Like she wasn't just inches away from me, like we weren't just about to—

"Earth to Will." Chase's voice breaks through. "We running that bridge again?"

"Yeah." I adjust my in-ears, trying to focus. "Yeah, let's do it."

Raine's voice comes through my headphones, cool and controlled. "Recording. Take one."

But her finger stays on the talkback button a fraction too long.

And when I glance up, she's watching me instead of the meters. Our eyes meet for a split second, and we both look away quickly.

I don't know what just happened between us. If anything. Maybe I imagined the whole thing. But I couldn't have. Not with how she's reacting too.

Could she possibly feel...?

I shake my head, scattering those thoughts. I know better than to hope for something like that. It's too fantastic to believe. Not after all this time.

*But then...why did she jump away so quickly like that?*

The morning crawls by in fits and starts. Every time I nail a take, her "that's the one" comes through just a beat too quick, like she's been waiting to speak. Like she's as aware of me as I am of her.

Chase keeps looking between us, but for once he keeps his mouth shut. Maybe Eliza's finally teaching him subtlety. Or maybe he just recognizes the tension in the room - the kind that makes you afraid to strike a match.

"Let's break for coffee," Raphael suggests after a particularly rough take. My timing's off, distracted by the way Raine tucks her hair behind her ear when she's thinking. By how she keeps almost meeting my eyes through the glass, then looking away.

"I'll get it." Mark's already heading for the door. "Usual for everyone?"

Raine stands quickly. "I'll help carry."

"I got it," I say at the same time.

Chase snorts softly. "Yeah, that's not obvious at all."

But Raine's already slipped into the hallway, and I'm still sitting at my kit like an idiot, watching her go. Again.

Through the control room window, Raphael raises an eyebrow at me.

Some things you can't hide behind sound-proofed glass.

No matter how hard you try.

Raphael follows Mark and Raine, probably

sensing the need for air in the room. Chase lingers, fiddling with his bass string.

"So," he says carefully. "You want to talk about it?"

"About what?" I focus on adjusting my kick pedal. Again.

"About whatever happened before we got here." He sets his bass down. "About why you both looked like teenagers caught behind the bleachers when we walked in."

"Nothing happened."

"Right." He drops into a chair. "That's why you're blushing like a drummer who got caught checking the mic placements way too close to his ex-wife."

I start to protest, but he holds up a hand. "Look, I'm the last person who should give advice about complicated relationships—"

"There's no relationship."

"Says the guy who brings her coffee creamer at ten PM."

My head snaps up. "How did you—"

"Maya tells Eliza everything. And Eliza..." He grins. "Well, let's just say sobriety has made me a better listener."

Through the hall window, I catch a glimpse of Raine walking back with Mark, her head bent close as they talk. She's probably telling him nothing happened, too. Probably trying to convince herself as well as him.

"Twenty years, Will." Chase's voice is gentle. "That's how long I wasted pretending Eliza and I were just keeping things casual."

"This is different."

"Yeah." He stands, picking up his bass again. "This is worse. Because at least Eliza and I admitted we had feelings. You two are still pretending you don't see what everyone else does."

The others file back in before I can respond. Raine hands me a coffee - black, two sugars, same as always - without quite meeting my eyes. She's extra careful not to let our fingers touch.

"Ready?" Her voice comes through my headphones, steady and professional once more.

I tap my snare twice. Ready.

Even if we both know it's a lie.

I'm not ready. For any of this.

*Am I?*

# *Mud*

~~~

RAINE

I **HEAR** them before I see them - Will offering production suggestions while Lucas plays back a track. They're both so focused they don't notice me in the doorway. Will's got that intense look he gets when he's onto something musically, jacket off, sleeves rolled up, leaning into the speakers.

"Now, hear how the drums sit in the new mix?" He gestures at the console. "The way they—"

"Mom!" Lucas spots me. "You're early."

Will's hand freezes mid-gesture. We haven't seen each other since this morning's near kiss at his band's studio.

"Deadline moved up." I hold up the hard drive with today's vocal sessions. "Label wants final vocals by Thursday. Some big promo push next week before the tour."

"Wait, before you start." Lucas spins his chair

around. "Listen to something. Here's how we've been playing it..."

He pulls up their new single. The one they've been working on all week. It's solid - exactly what we tracked. The drums drive the track forward, Lucas's signature style clear in the intricate fills.

"Dad dropped by earlier, thought something felt off. Here's what we just worked out..."

The new version starts. The difference hits immediately. The drums pull back in the verses, creating space for the vocal line to breathe. In the chorus, Lucas's fills weave through the gaps instead of competing with the melody. It's the kind of subtle adjustment that comes from years of experience - or from growing up watching your father learn these lessons the hard way.

"The ghost notes in the bridge," I say, professional mode engaging. "They're supporting the vocal rhythm now instead of fighting it."

Will's watching me listen, that familiar tension in his jaw when he's trying not to look proud of something. "Sometimes less is more."

"That's what you said during the first album sessions, too." The words slip out before I can stop them. "When we spent three days reworking the drum patterns for 'Midnight Rain.'"

Lucas glances between us, clearly noting the weight of that memory. "I should get these changes bounced before tomorrow's session."

"Right." I move toward the console, reaching for my laptop. "I've got six hours of vocals to sort through anyway. The label wants two singles ready for the promo tour, plus B-sides for the international release."

"That's a lot of comping," Will says, still watching me. "Even for you."

"Good thing I'm the best." I pull up the first session file. "And someone once kept me company through endless vocal takes, back when we were just starting out."

"That someone had ulterior motives," Will says softly, then seems to catch himself. "For the good of the album, I mean."

Lucas coughs, hiding what sounds suspiciously like a laugh. "These files are rendering. Should be done in a few minutes."

I focus on setting up my session template, trying not to think about those early recording days. About Will bringing me coffee at midnight, claiming he just happened to be working late, too. About the way every technical discussion somehow turned into something more.

"The harmony stack in the second verse needs the most work," Lucas says, pulling me back to the present. "We tried about six different approaches today."

"I heard the rough takes." I scan through the files.

"You've got good instincts, but the third layer's fighting with the lead."

"That's what I was saying," Will moves closer to the screen. "If you just—"

He stops, suddenly aware of how near he is. This morning floods back - the empty studio, his arm brushing mine, that charged moment before the others arrived.

"I should head out." Lucas stands, far too casual about gathering his things. "Let you pros handle the vocal production."

"You don't have to—" Will starts.

"No, really." Lucas shoulders his bag, then kisses my cheek. "Don't work too late, Mom."

The studio feels smaller once he's gone. Just me and Will and the weight of everything we're not discussing. Just his presence in the same room with me makes my pulse race, and my stomach flip. Even when we were apart, even when we were married to other people.

Even now.

Maybe *especially* now.

"The label's really pushing this deadline?" Will asks from his spot by the console, still not quite looking at me.

"Thursday delivery." I pull up the first session, organizing vocal takes into folders. "They want the press cut by Monday. Some morning show performance next week, then the Asian promo tour starts."

"That's a lot of vocals to comp in two days."

"Ninety-six tracks just from today's session." I try for casual, professional. "Plus harmonies, doubles, backing vocals..."

"No wonder you're here late." He shifts, that nervous energy from this morning still visible in his hands. "I remember when you used to mark all the good takes in red. Color coding every possible option."

"I still do." I pull up a track, showing him my system. "Red for keepers, yellow for maybes. Just like—"

"Our first album." He moves closer to see the screen. "Three AM, ordering Chinese food, arguing about that one note in the bridge..."

"We weren't always arguing about the note." The words slip out before I can stop myself. I really need to just shut the hell up.

His sharp inhale tells me he remembers, too - how those late-night sessions usually ended. How technical discussions about harmony and pitch turned into something else entirely.

How we almost kissed this morning.

"Actually..." He steps back slightly, keys jingling in his hand. "I was going to grab coffee early tomorrow, before the session. Go over those drum tracks for the bridge section. If you wanted to..."

My hands still on the keyboard. This morning's almost-moment flashes back - the empty studio, the brush of his fingers through my hair, the way time stopped until Chase and Mark arrived. The same electricity that's been building since Friday's session. Since he showed up at my door with coffee creamer.

"Just coffee," he adds quickly. "Professional discussion."

"Professional." I meet his eyes finally. "Like this morning?"

His fingers tap against his keys - the same nervous rhythm from when we were recording earlier. "Seven?"

"The Standard?" I turn back to my screen, needing to look at anything else. Anything but him in all his stupid handsomeness just feet away. The waveforms blur slightly as I try to focus on labeling tracks, on my system, on anything but the way the studio feels way too small suddenly.

He nods, finally moving toward the door. Then stops. "You'll be okay? Working late?"

The real question lies beneath - will I be okay alone? Will I notice when he drives by later to check? Will either of us admit what all these little moments are adding up to?

"I'm good." My voice stays steady somehow, despite my nerves dancing in chaos. "Just vocals to comp. Ninety-six tracks worth."

"Raine..."

"I know. Thanks, though."

Then he's gone, and I'm alone with hours of vocal

tracks to sort through. Professional. Focused. Not thinking about early morning coffee or charged silences or the way he still worries. Not thinking about how tomorrow morning will be just us again, no kids or bandmates as buffers.

I stare at the screen, at my careful color-coding system. Red for keepers. Yellow for maybes. No color for the way my heart still speeds up when he's near, for the growing collection of almost-moments between us, for the fact that we're running out of professional excuses to be alone together.

Just work to do.

Even if every harmony makes me think about tomorrow morning, and how nothing between us has ever been "just" anything.

## WILL

**THE STANDARD COFFEE BAR.** That's what they call it now, all exposed brick and pour-over stations. Twenty-four years ago, it was just Joe's, with sticky formica tables and coffee that could strip paint. Raine used to joke that's why all our early vocals were so raw - caffeine damage.

I'm early, watching them set up for the morning rush. Our old corner's been replaced by some kind of manual brewing station, but the window seat where we used to work out harmony arrangements is still here. Different table. Same view.

"The usual?" The older barista's already starting my drink. Black coffee's apparently too simple now - they call it a "dark roast pour over." Raine's vanilla latte probably has a fancy name, too.

"And a—" I start.

"Grande vanilla latte, extra hot?" She grins knowingly. "Your wife's usually here later. Actually, I haven't seen you two here together in forever…"

"Ex-wife." The correction comes automatically. "And she'll be here soon."

The barista raises an eyebrow but doesn't comment. Now that I actually pay attention, I think she used to work here when it was Joe's. I don't know how I never noticed that.

I hear Raine's car before I see her. Still driving that Mercedes E-class. Some things don't change, even if the coffee shop's unrecognizable, and our kids are grown, and we're meeting at seven AM to discuss drum patterns we could easily talk about at the studio.

Hell, this entire meeting is unnecessary, and I'm sure we both know it.

She pauses in the doorway, taking in the changes. Her eyes find me immediately - some internal compass that hasn't failed in twenty-million years. The morning light catches the silver threading through her dark hair, subtle highlights that only make her more elegant. She moves through the now-crowded space with that same grace that used to command stages, that now commands studios.

"They've certainly upgraded," she says, sliding into the seat across from me. When she tucks her hair behind her ear - that nervous tell she's never lost - I catch the faint scent of her perfume. Still vanilla, still making it hard to focus.

"Remember that ancient drip machine Joe used to have?" She accepts the latte I push toward her.

"The one that exploded during final mixing?" I watch her wrap both hands around the cup, gathering warmth like she always has. "Chase still claims it was sabotage from the studio down the street. Thanks for remembering my order, by the way."

"Of course. Some things stick." Like how she still sits with her back to the wall, old performer's habit. Like how I still notice every detail about her without meaning to. "Though apparently, it's an 'artisanal vanilla bean latte' now."

She laughs softly. "Very artisanal. Very seven AM."

"And, actually," I whisper conspiratorially, glancing at the counter, "the barista remembers you, too."

Raine leans in as well, part of the conspiracy, her hair falls forward and it takes everything in me not to reach out and tuck it behind her ear like I did yesterday.

"Oh, really?" she whispers back. "What did she say?" She raises her hand to her face, pretending to peek at the counter surreptitiously.

It's only then that I realize what I have to tell her. *Shit.*

I swallow hard, trying to keep it light. "She called you my wife."

A range of emotions flow over Raine's face as she

pulls back. Surprise, disbelief, and is that a touch of sadness I see?

"Well," she says, straightening, quickly putting on a neutral mask I know so well. "I hope you corrected her."

My heart sinks slightly at her response. But then, what did I expect? Her to be happy that people still think we're married after all this time? It's kind of ridiculous.

It throws my emotions into a tailspin wondering what we're even doing here now.

The unspoken questions hang between us. Why here? Why now? Why not wait two hours and discuss Lucas's drums at the studio like professionals?

"So." She takes a careful sip, clearly avoiding looking at me. "The tour routing came through last night."

"Both bands together." I try to sound casual. "Chase's idea."

"Of course it was." Her brown eyes spark with knowing amusement. "Nothing to do with you wanting to keep an eye on Lucas?"

"Can't a father watch his son's first major arena tour?"

"Like you're not going to text me detailed reports after every show." She sets down her cup, motherly pride warring with concern. "The same way you called me from every city when he was learning to drive."

"That was different." I focus on my coffee. "He was sixteen."

"And now he's twenty-two, opening at Madison Square Garden for Incendiary Ink." Her voice carries the same mix of pride and worry I feel every time I think about it. "Playing bigger venues than you did at his age."

"It's not just the venues." I watch her trace the rim of her cup, that familiar gesture when she's choosing her words carefully. "Last night at his session... he's so focused. So ready. Almost too ready."

"You're worried he's pushing too hard?" The morning light catches the silver in her hair again as she leans forward. "Will, you should hear him in the studio when you're not there. The way he works with the other guys, how he handles himself in production meetings. He's not that kid lugging his practice pad to every family dinner anymore."

"No, he's not." Pride mixes with something else - maybe grief for that eager kid, maybe fear for the man taking his place. "But the road... it changes people, Raine. You've seen it happen. The grind, the pressure, the constant—"

"He's not you," she says gently. "And Another Angel isn't Incendiary Ink. The industry's different now. Support's better. Hell, these kids have wellness coaches and nutritionists."

"Yeah." I study her face. "The nutritionist worked

with their catering team. Got all the meal timing worked out."

She nods, understanding the real message. "And the supplies?"

"Extra CGM sensors and insulin in three different places. Plus, everyone knows the drill by now. It's going to be up to Lucas to manage, though."

"Good." Her fingers tighten slightly on her cup. "After that session last month..."

"That was different. He just lost track of time in the studio."

"Again - like father, like son," she says, but there's worry beneath the teasing. We both remember too many nights of him pushing himself too hard, forgetting to eat, his numbers crashing during rehearsals.

"And he has two parents who've lived this life." My hand moves toward hers before I can stop it. "Who know what to watch for."

She doesn't pull away, and my chest tightens at the feel of her skin against mine. "Like someone watching out for midnight drive-bys?"

I ignore the comment, not wanting to dive into things too personal for some reason. The morning rush starts building even more around us. Students with laptops, executives grabbing drinks before meetings. The intimate bubble of early morning beginning to fade.

"The tour buses are better now, too," I say, changing the subject, reaching for safer ground but not quite ready to move my hand. I'm afraid to move it. To sever the connection. "Actually have shock absorption. Real bunks."

"Unlike that death trap you used to tour in? The one that broke down in every state?" Her lips quirk into a half-smile.

"Only the western states." I can't help smiling back at the memory. "Though Chase swears Nebraska was trying to keep us."

"At least Lucas won't have to deal with that." She pulls her hand away finally, and glances at her watch - almost time for the session. Almost time to go back to being professional. "First class all the way. The label's really backing them."

"Yeah." I study her face, seeing the same concern I feel. "It's different now. Better."

"But?"

"But he's still going to be out there. Living that life." The one that cost us everything. The one I'm about to jump back into myself. "I just want to..."

"Watch over him?" Her voice softens. "Make sure he's okay?"

I can only nod, knowing she's talking about me as well. Like I've been doing with late-night drive-bys and coffee creamer deliveries.

I guess I'm not as subtle as I think I am.

"We should head to the studio." She stands, gathering her things. Professional mask sliding back into place. "The others will be waiting."

"Raine." My hand catches hers again before I can stop myself. "About yesterday..."

Her hand stills under mine. The morning bustle fades away, and suddenly we're alone in this moment, in this transformed coffee shop that somehow still holds echoes of who we used to be.

"Will." Her voice is barely audible. "We can't..."

"I know." But I don't let go. Don't want to let go. "I just... when you're working late. If you need anything..."

"Like coffee creamer?" The ghost of a smile plays at her lips.

"Or drum pattern advice." I try to match her light tone. "Professional courtesy."

"Right." She gently withdraws her hand, but her eyes hold mine. "Professional."

Like this morning's coffee was professional. Like last night's studio tension was professional. Like every moment since Lucas's showcase has been anything close to professional.

"The others will be wondering..." She shoulders her bag, all business now. "Chase is probably already making up stories about where we are."

"Let him." The words slip out before I can stop them.

She pauses, that familiar catch in her breath that I've been trying not to notice since Friday. "Will..."

"I know." I stand, reaching for my jacket. For the safety of movement, of preparation to leave. "Just..."

"Just coffee," she finishes softly.

Outside, the morning sun hits the brick buildings, making everything look softer, older. When she reaches for her keys, I catch that trace of vanilla again - from her latte, from her perfume, from the creamer I brought last night. All these small details I can't seem to stop noticing.

"I'll follow you," she says, gesturing to her car. Then stops, realizing how that sounds. "To the studio, I mean."

"Right." I shift my keys between hands. "The studio."

Neither of us moves.

A delivery truck backs into the coffee shop's loading zone, breaking the moment. The real world crashing back in. In minutes we'll be in the studio, maintaining careful distance across the console. Professional. Appropriate. Not thinking about this morning or last night or how many more excuses we can find to be alone together.

"Will?" She pauses at her car door. "About Lucas. And the tour."

"Yeah?"

"Maybe..." She takes a careful breath. "Maybe we could get coffee again? Go over the routing, figure out which shows we'll both be at. For Lucas."

"For Lucas," I echo. "Professional planning."

"Exactly." But her smile holds something else. Something that makes my heart beat like I'm young again, watching her perform for the first time. "Tomorrow?"

"Tomorrow."

I watch her get in her car, thinking about transformed coffee shops and unchanged feelings. About how some things evolve - pour-over stations and artisanal lattes - while others stay exactly the same.

Like the way my hands still remember her touch, even after all these years.

Like how nothing between us has ever really been just coffee.

# Silent Stranger

## RAINE

**WILL'S** car makes a right onto Sunset, the familiar route to Blackmore. I keep three cars between us, like I'm tailing a suspect in some noir film instead of following my ex-husband from a coffee meeting that was supposed to be about drum patterns. A coffee meeting that somehow turned into plans for tomorrow's coffee. And probably the next day's. And the day after that.

Just professional discussion.

*Right.*

The Mercedes's climate control is perfect, but I can still feel the ghost of morning chill where his hand touched mine. Still hear the way his voice changed when he said, "tomorrow." Twenty-million years of history packed into one word.

He signals left into the studio lot. I wait two beats before following, giving us both space to compose ourselves before facing the others. Before pretending that coffee was just coffee and tomorrow is just another day.

My hands shake slightly as I gather my things. The same hands that used to be steady in any session, any situation. The same hands that trembled that night when he brought coffee creamer to my door.

"You're late." Chase's voice carries across the parking lot. He's leaning against the back entrance, green smoothie in hand. "Both of you."

I check my watch. "Session's not for twenty minutes."

"Funny." His grin is knowing. "You're usually an hour early. Will too."

"Traffic." Will appears from his car, all business now. Professional distance restored.

But Chase just sips his smoothie, eyes dancing between us. "Right. Traffic."

The studio feels different this morning. Smaller. Every brush past each other charged with new awareness as we set up. Will adjusts mic stands with too much focus while I pretend to review charts I memorized days ago.

"Where's Mark?" I ask, desperate for buffer conversation.

"Parking." Chase settles behind the console. "Something about his bike acting up. Though if you two need more time to discuss... traffic..."

"The drum pattern in the bridge—" Will starts.

"Really?" Chase sets down his smoothie. "That's what you're going with?"

"Chase." My warning tone is automatic, same one I use when Lucas pushes too hard in sessions.

"Fine." He holds up his hands in mock surrender. "We'll pretend you weren't just having coffee together."

Will's hands still on the kick drum mic. I focus very hard on my session notes, on anything except the way the morning sun catches his profile through the control room window. The way he looked at me with hope in his eyes when he said, "tomorrow."

"Morning, children!" Mark breezes in, blue mohawk slightly windblown. "Everyone survive the traffic?"

Chase snorts into his smoothie.

"Let's run the chorus." I reach for the talkback, grateful for the distraction. "Chase, try that harmony we worked out yesterday."

"Sure." His tone is too innocent.

I ignore him, focusing on levels. On frequencies. On anything except the memory of Will's hand on mine at the coffee shop. The way neither of us pulled away. Until I had to when I couldn't take it anymore.

"Recording." My voice stays steady somehow despite every single nerve being on edge. "Take one."

The music starts, and for a moment, everything else fades. This is what I'm good at - taking separate pieces and making them whole. Guitar and bass and drums weaving together while Chase's voice soars over it all. Adding bits of myself to the mix, building something bigger than any one piece.

But then Will shifts his vocal pattern slightly, opening space for the lead exactly like we discussed over coffee. Like he's still trying to prove he remembers everything I taught him about letting harmony breathe.

"That's the one." I try to sound neutral. Appropriate. "Unless you need another pass?"

"That was perfect." Chase grins through the glass. "Almost like you two already worked it out. Over coffee, maybe?"

"The harmonies in the pre-chorus..." I start, but Will's already nodding, already adjusting his headphones. Already knowing exactly what I mean, like he always has.

"One more." His voice comes through my headphones, steady and sure. "From the bridge?"

I count them in, trying not to notice how his timing matches my breathing. How easily we fall into old rhythms, despite everything we're not talking about. Despite tomorrow's coffee hanging between us like an unresolved chord.

Mark's track launches into the bridge riff, and Chase's voice blends with mine in perfect thirds. But all I can hear is Will's subtle adjustment of the groove, the way he's anticipating every vocal nuance. Reading me like sheet music he's memorized.

"Nice." Raphael appears in the doorway. "Though the vocals in the last chorus..."

"Need to come up a half step." Will finishes before I can. Our eyes meet through the glass, and for a moment everything else disappears.

"Exactly what I was going to say." Raphael glances between us. "Good to see you two... in sync again."

Chase makes a sound that might be a laugh disguised as a cough.

"Let's take five." Raphael's voice breaks the moment. "Coffee break."

"More coffee?" Mark raises an eyebrow. "Some of us already had plenty this morning."

I busy myself with the console, pretending to adjust settings that don't need adjusting. Through the glass, Will's doing the same with his kit, head down, hands moving with careful precision.

"Actually," Chase stands, stretching. "I need Raphael's opinion on that bass line in the outro. Mark?"

They file out, leaving Will and me alone again. The silence fills with everything we're not saying. With coffee shop memories still fresh. With tomorrow's promises.

After several long minutes, he moves to the control room door. Pauses. "About tomorrow..."

"Professional discussion." I keep my eyes on the board. "About drum patterns and tour schedules."

"Right." His voice is closer now. "Just like today was professional."

I look up. Mistake. He's standing right next to me, watching me with that intensity that's always undone me. That's made me rework entire arrangements just to match what I see in his blue eyes.

"Will—"

The door opens. Chase again, timing perfect as always. "We ready to work? Or should we give you two more time to discuss... patterns?"

"The vocals need..." Will starts.

"Don't." Chase holds up a hand. "Just don't. Twenty-five years of friendship means I know when you're both trying too hard to seem professional." He looks between us. "Something's different. Since Friday. Since the weekend. Since this morning's coffee that we're all pretending wasn't a thing."

"Chase." Will's warning tone is familiar.

"Fine." He settles back at his mic. "Let's work. Let's all pretend we don't see what's happening. Again."

I reach for the talkback button, grateful for the return to session routine. But Will's still in the doorway, still watching me with that look that makes it hard to remember why we're pretending at all.

"From the bridge?" My voice sounds steadier than I feel.

He nods once, finally moving back to his booth. But his eyes hold mine through the glass a moment too long. Professional distance cracking just enough to let something else show through.

Something that tastes like vanilla lattes and feels like tomorrow's promises.

"Recording." I focus on the console. On the music. On anything except the way every harmony seems to lead back to him. "Take seven."

"About tomorrow—" he starts.

"Professional," I remind us both.

"Professional." But his smile holds something else. Something that makes me forget about more Netflix deadlines and careful distance and all the reasons we're supposed to be just colleagues now.

I need to be so, so careful.

# *Breaking Inside*

## WILL

"THAT'S THE ONE." Raine's voice comes through my headphones, professional as ever. Like this morning's coffee never happened. Like we haven't been dancing around each other all day. "Unless anyone needs another pass?"

"We're good." Chase starts packing up his bass. "Some of us have actual lives outside the studio."

Mark snorts. "Says the guy planning a wedding with the label president."

I'm coiling cables, pretending I don't feel Raine's eyes on me every time she reaches for the console. Pretending this is just another session. Just another day.

"Dad?" Lucas appears in the doorway, fresh from Another Angel's rehearsal down the hall. "Got a minute?"

"Sure." I set down the cables, grateful for the distraction. "Everything okay?"

"Yeah, just..." He glances around the studio. "The label added some dates. Between the Incendiary Ink shows."

The room goes quiet. Even Chase stops packing.

"What kind of dates?" Raine's voice is careful. Controlled.

"Television. Some industry showcases." Lucas pulls out his phone. "Plus a few headlining slots when Incendiary Ink has breaks in routing."

"Let me see that schedule." I move toward him, but Raine's already pulling up the calendar on the console monitor. Our eyes meet briefly - same worry, different angles.

"We should head out." Chase's voice is unusually gentle. Understanding. "Early meeting tomorrow."

Mark follows his lead. "Yeah, I've got... something."

Lucas hands me his phone. "I can stay, go over the details—"

"No." Raine's tone is motherly but firm. "You've got that interview in the morning. Get some rest."

They file out, leaving us alone with tour schedules and shared concerns. The studio feels different now - more intimate without the buffer of the band. Without the pretense of professional distance.

I settle next to her at the console, close enough to

see the calendar but not quite touching. "These dates in Chicago...Cleveland...Pittsburgh..."

"Back-to-back shows in different venues." She zooms in on the schedule. "No real recovery time."

"We'll need to talk to the road manager about—"

"Medical staff at both locations," she finishes. "And proper breaks between sound checks."

Her arm brushes mine as she reaches for the mouse. Neither of us moves.

"The routing's tight." Her voice is softer now, less producer and more mother. "Three shows in four days, then straight to the Incendiary Ink dates."

"He can handle it." But I'm not sure who I'm trying to convince.

"Will." Just my name, but it carries the weight of years. Of shared worry and midnight hospital visits and learning to trust our son's judgment.

I turn to face her, to offer some reassurance, but she's already looking at me. Close enough to catch that trace of vanilla that's been driving me crazy all day. Close enough to see the flecks of gold in her eyes now that appear when she's unsettled, the slight tremor in her hands as she reaches for the mouse again.

"We should..." Her voice trails off as my hand covers hers on the console.

The studio goes quiet except for the hum of equipment. The same console where we recorded our first album. Where she used to perch while I worked out drum patterns. Where everything started, all those years ago.

"Raine."

She turns toward me, and suddenly there's no air in the room. No space between us. No professional distance left to hide behind.

Our eyes meet, and twenty-four years disappear. She's that club singer again, teaching me about vocal space. I'm that eager drummer, trying to impress her with my timing. Everything we've been avoiding since the showcase crystalizes in this moment.

I lean in slowly, giving her time to pull away. Her eyes flutter closed, and I feel her breath catch. Just inches between us now. The scent of vanilla. The warmth of her hand under mine.

"Wait." She pulls back suddenly, standing. "We can't... This is..."

"Professional?" The word tastes bitter now.

"I should go." She starts gathering her things, movements too quick, too jerky. "It's late."

"Raine—"

"Coffee tomorrow?" Her voice shakes slightly. "To discuss the tour schedule?"

"Right." I stand too, needing space to breathe. To think. "Professional discussion."

She pauses at the door. "Will you...?"

"I'll follow you home." Like always. Like every night since she moved to my neighborhood. "Make sure you're safe."

The look she gives me holds everything we're not saying. Everything we almost did.

"Tomorrow then."

I watch her Mercedes ahead of me on Sunset, both of us knowing this drive is different from my usual security checks. Both of us aware that tomorrow's coffee won't be professional at all.

She signals right, toward her condo. I maintain my distance - three cars between us, like always. But tonight the space feels charged. Heavy with almost-kisses and vanilla perfume and years of muscle memory neither of us can seem to forget.

Her brake lights illuminate as she pulls into her drive. I slow to a stop, watching her gather her things. Making sure she gets inside safe. That's what I tell myself. That's what we both pretend.

She pauses at her door, key in hand, and looks back toward my car. For a moment, I think she might wave me in. Might ask me to come check her locks, or chat, like I did that night with the coffee creamer.

Instead, she gives a small nod. An acknowledgment. A promise, maybe.

*Tomorrow.*

I wait until her lights come on, until I know she's secure. Then I drive home the long way, past the coffee shop where we'll meet in nine hours.

Nine hours. But who's counting?

I am. I'm fucking counting.

# Everything I Need

I'M on my second latte before Will arrives. Not that I'm worrying. Not that I've been here since they opened, watching the door, replaying the past week in my head. The almost-kiss. The way he followed me home. The weight of everything we're not really pretending anymore.

He pauses in the doorway, and for a moment it's like looking through time. Same careful stance, same way of watching me like he's memorizing every detail. Same flutter in my chest that no amount of professional distance can quiet.

"You're early." His tall frame settles across from me, closer than yesterday.

"Couldn't sleep." The truth slips out before I can catch it.

"Yeah." He studies his coffee. "Me neither."

The morning rush builds around us, but our corner

feels separate. Intimate. Like we're in our own time zone where nothing exists except this moment. This conversation we can't avoid anymore.

"Will—"

"About last night—"

We both stop. Start again.

"You first," I manage, spinning my cup nervously on the table.

"I've been trying to keep this professional." His fingers tap against his cup, that nervous rhythm I still recognize. "Trying to pretend coffee is just coffee and studio sessions are just work."

"How's that going for you?" The question comes out softer than I meant it to.

"About as well as it's going for you." His eyes meet mine. Intense. Hopeful. "You pulled away last night."

"I did." I wrap both hands around my cup, needing something to hold onto. "Because once we cross that line..."

"Everything changes."

"Again." I take a careful breath. "Will, the tour starts in three weeks. Lucas has all these new dates. The album deadline—"

"I know." He leans forward slightly, and I catch a whiff of his cologne. Spicy and sweet at the same time. It's intoxicating. "I know all the reasons why this is complicated. Why we should keep our distance. Stay professional."

"But?"

"But I still drive by your condo every night. Still worry about you, your security. Still catch myself watching you in the studio like I'm twenty-five again, trying to impress you with my timing."

The honesty in his voice makes my hands shake. I set down my cup before he notices.

"We're not twenty-five anymore," I say quietly. "We have careers, responsibilities. A son about to tour—"

"Who needs both his parents focused and clear-headed." He nods. "I know. But Raine..." His hand moves toward mine, stops. "Being professional isn't making me any more focused. Is it working for you?"

"No." The admission feels like relief. Like finally exhaling after holding my breath since the showcase. "But we can't just..."

"Jump back in? No." His smile is gentle. Understanding. Mature. "We're not kids anymore. We know better."

"Do we?" I think about last night. About how easily we fall into old patterns. Old feelings that maybe aren't so old after all.

"I think..." He pauses, choosing his words carefully. "I think we know what we lost now. What matters. What doesn't."

"The tour life broke us once." But even as I say it, I know that's not the whole truth.

"*We* broke us," he corrects softly. "The tour was just the excuse."

The morning bustle fades away as his words sink in. He's right. We were young, scared of what we had, of what we could lose. Easier to blame distance and schedules than admit we didn't know how to handle something that big.

That *real*.

"Lucas wants to talk to both of us later," I say. "About the new dates."

"I know." Will's voice stays gentle. "But that's not what we're really talking about, is it?"

"No." I meet his eyes finally. "It's not."

"So let's be honest. Finally." He leans forward again, and I'm wrapped the scent of his cologne, entranced by his gaze, unable to look away even if I wanted to. "I miss you. Not just professionally. Not just as Maya and Lucas's mom. I miss us."

My breath catches. "Will—"

"And I think... I think maybe you miss us too."

The truth of it hits like a tidal wave. "I do." My voice barely carries. "But that terrifies me."

"Good." His smile is soft. "Because it terrifies me, too. And maybe that's the difference this time. Maybe being scared means we'll be more careful with it."

"Careful." I test the word. "Like taking it slow?"

"Like seeing where this goes. No pressure." His hand covers mine finally. It's warm and a little shaky. "Just coffee that's actually coffee. Dinner, maybe.

Real conversations instead of pretending we're just colleagues."

"While still being professional at work?" But I don't pull my hand away. Not only can't I, but I don't want to this time.

"During sessions, yes." He squeezes my fingers gently, his fingers rough with callouses that bring back so many memories. "But after hours..."

"The tour starts in three weeks," I remind him.

"I know. And we'll figure that out. Together." His thumb traces circles on my palm. "But right now... right now I'd just like to have coffee with you. *Really* have coffee with you. No pretense."

"And the kids?"

"We tell them when we're sure. When we know what *this* is." He pauses. "If that's what you want?"

The question hangs between us. Everything we've been avoiding since the showcase. Since my divorce. Maybe since our own divorce, if I'm being honest.

"Yes," I whisper. Then stronger: "Yes. But slow."

His smile makes my heart skip like I'm twenty-four again, watching him practice drum patterns just to spend time with me.

"Slow," he agrees. "Though maybe we should define that. Since our track record with 'professional' hasn't been great."

"No studio moments." I try to sound firm despite his thumb still tracing patterns on my palm.

"No late night planning sessions alone?"

"Definitely not." But I'm smiling now too. "And no using Lucas's tour schedule as an excuse to see each other."

"Even if we're legitimately worried about the routing?"

"We can discuss that over coffee." I gesture at our cups. "In public places. With plenty of witnesses."

His laugh is soft, intimate. "Like proper adults?"

"Exactly." I squeeze his hand once before pulling back. "We do this right this time. No rushing. No assumptions."

"Starting with...?"

"Dinner." The word surprises us both. "Tonight? Somewhere nice. Not Salvatore's."

"A real date." His blue eyes light up. "I'll pick you up at seven?"

"I'll meet you there," I correct, trying to keep my heart from pounding out of my chest. "Slow, remember?"

He stands, gathering his things for the studio session ahead. "Tonight then. But Raine?"

"Hmm?"

"Just so we're clear - I'm still driving by to check your house. Some habits aren't negotiable."

I watch him leave, thinking about habits and second chances and how some rhythms never really fade. But maybe, just maybe, that's not such a bad thing.

As long as we take it slow.

# Nervous

## WILL

**OTIUM ISN'T** our usual type of place. No worn leather booths, no classic rock soundtrack, no comfortable routine of family dinners and shop talk. The hostess leads me to a quiet corner table, all sleek lines and ambient lighting. Everything about tonight says *different. New. Intentional.*

I check my watch. Ten minutes early, but I'm betting she is too. Some habits don't change, even if everything else has.

Movement at the door catches my eye. Raine, in a dark blue dress I've never seen, her dark hair loose around her shoulders. Different from studio Raine, from co-parent Raine. From any version of her I've been pretending not to notice lately.

She still takes my breath away.

She spots me immediately - that internal compass that's never failed - and for a moment we're both frozen. Taking in this new reality we've chosen. This careful step toward something we're both afraid to name.

"You look..." The words catch in my throat.

"Different?" She settles across from me, smoothing her dress nervously. "I wasn't sure about—"

"Perfect." The truth slips out, but I don't even care. "You look perfect."

A slight blush colors her cheeks. For a moment we're both tongue-tied, like teenagers on a first date instead of adults with decades of history between us.

"Nice choice." She glances around the restaurant, her keen eyes probably noticing everything. "No chance of running into anyone from the industry here."

"That was the idea." I resist the urge to reach for her hand. Slow, we agreed. "Though Chase offered several suggestions."

"Of course he did." Her laugh eases some of the tension. "Let me guess - all places with convenient dark corners?"

"And convenient exits if we need to escape the awkwardness."

"Is it?" She meets my eyes. And I sense her apprehension, her fear. "Awkward?"

"No." The answer comes quickly, certainly. "That's what scares me."

The waiter appears with menus, giving us both a

moment to breathe. To adjust to this new dynamic where we're not pretending anymore. Where coffee isn't just coffee and dinner isn't just dinner.

"Wine?" I offer, though I already know her preference. Some details you don't forget.

"Please." She studies the menu, but I catch her stealing glances. Like she's checking if this feels as surreal to me as it does to her.

The sommelier appears, and for a few minutes we're safe in the routine of ordering. But once we're alone again, the weight of everything we're not saying settles back around us.

"This morning," she starts carefully. Too carefully. "In the studio..."

"We were professional." I managed to keep my distance all day, even if every fiber of my being was aware of her presence. "Like we agreed."

"We were." A small smile plays at her lips. "Though Chase kept giving us looks."

"Chase always gives looks." I lean forward slightly. "But that's not what you want to talk about."

She takes a careful sip of wine. "No. It's not."

"Raine." Her name comes out softer than I intended; more gravely and emotional. "We don't have to figure everything out tonight."

"Don't we?" Her eyes meet mine over her glass, and I can sense her worry. "Three weeks until tour. The album deadline. Lucas's schedule..."

"We spent years trying to figure everything out." I

reach for her hand, unable to help myself. "Making plans. Being practical. Look how well that worked."

Her fingers curl into mine automatically. "So, what's your suggestion?"

"Right now? I'd like to have dinner with you. Just dinner." My thumb traces her knuckles. "Maybe tell you how beautiful you look. How much I've missed this."

"Will..."

"And maybe admit that I've been going crazy all day, wanting to tell you that this morning's coffee was the best I've had in thirteen years."

A soft laugh escapes her. "Because of the artisanal roast?"

"Because you were really there. Not just Lucas's mom or the vocal producer or my ex-wife. Just *you*."

The waiter appears with our first course, and Raine starts to pull her hand away. I hold on for just a moment longer.

"Stay," I whisper. "Just... stay."

She leaves her hand in mine while the waiter sets down our plates. Like we've made some unspoken agreement. Like we're done pretending.

"I've missed this too," she admits softly once we're alone again. "Not just... this." She squeezes my fingers. "But being able to look at you without worrying who might notice. Without having to be professional."

"Though you do professional very well." I can't help teasing. "All those vocal arrangements today..."

"Stop." But she's smiling. "I was trying so hard to focus."

"I know. Me too." I run my thumb across her palm, basking in the familiarity of the touch, as well as the newness. "Especially when you do that thing with your hair when you're concentrating."

"What thing?"

"The tucking it behind your ear. The way you've done since we met."

Her free hand moves automatically to her hair, and we both laugh. The tension eases, replaced by something warmer. Something that feels like coming home.

"Tell me something," she says, now intense. Now the *real* Raine. "Something real."

"I never got over you." The truth tumbles out on its own. My guard is completely down now. No more pretense. "Becca... that was me trying to move on. To be what everyone said I should be after the divorce."

Her hand tightens in mine. "Will..."

"I know we said slow." I meet her eyes again across the table. "And we should. We will. But I need you to know that. That none of it - not the second marriage, not the professional distance, not the careful co-parenting - none of it changed how I feel about you."

She's quiet for a long moment, her thumb tracing

patterns on my palm. "Eric wanted me to quit music," she says finally. "Said I had enough success, enough money. That it was time to be a proper wife."

"What did you tell him?"

"To fuck off," she giggles, and the sound is like music to my ears.

"Wow, really?" I laugh, picturing it perfectly in my mind.

"Well, no. Probably. I don't know. I told him that music isn't what I do. It's who I am." Her eyes find mine. "Just like you've always known. Even when we were falling apart, you never asked me to be less than I am."

"I just wanted you to be happy." The admission feels raw, honest. "I still do."

"And if being happy means taking a chance? Even with everything complicated ahead of us?"

"Then we take it one day at a time." I lean closer, drawn to her like always. "Figure it out together."

"The tour..." She starts, but I can see her resolve wavering.

"Will be different this time. We're different." I squeeze her hand gently. "We know what matters now."

"And what's that?"

"Being honest. With ourselves, with each other." I watch her process this. "No more hiding behind professional distance or careful boundaries. No more pretending that I don't still feel everything I felt twenty-four years ago."

The waiter appears with our entrees, but neither of us moves. The food can wait. This moment can't.

"I'm scared," she admits softly. "Of risking this. Of losing you again if it goes wrong."

"Good." I bring her hand to my lips, a ghost of a kiss against her knuckles. "Because that means it matters. That we'll be careful with it this time."

Her breath catches. "Will..."

"I know." I lower our hands but don't let go. "Slow. Public places. No studio moments."

"About that." A smile plays at her lips. "Maybe we can negotiate the studio rule. Eventually."

The possibility in her voice makes my heart race. "Eventually?"

"After we figure this out." She gestures between us with her free hand. "After we're sure."

"I'm already sure." The words come without hesitation. "Have been since the showcase. Since before that, if I'm honest."

She takes a careful breath. "The food's getting cold."

"Let it." But I release her hand, letting her set the pace. Letting her decide how much, how fast.

We eat in comfortable silence, stealing glances like teenagers. Everything feels different now. Charged with possibility. With promise.

"I should go soon." She checks her watch. "Early session tomorrow."

"I'll follow you home."

"Really?"

"Just to make sure you're safe." I signal for the check. "Professional concern."

Her laugh is worth every careful step, every moment of waiting. "Nothing about tonight has been professional. And to be honest, I'm getting sick of that word."

"Good. Me too."

The night air hits us as we step outside, carrying the scent of jasmine from the restaurant's courtyard. She lets me help her with her coat, and my fingers brush the bare skin of her neck. We both pretend not to notice how she shivers.

The walk to her car feels endless and too short at the same time. The click of her heels on pavement, the distant hum of traffic, the sound of my heart in my ears - everything amplified in this moment between dinner and goodbye.

At her Mercedes, she turns to face me, and suddenly the careful distance we've maintained all evening disappears. The streetlight catches the silver in her hair, the warmth in her eyes, and I'm twenty-five again, watching her sing *"Fever"* in that dive bar, knowing my life was about to change.

"Will—"

My name on her lips breaks the last thread of

restraint. When I kiss her, one hand sliding into her hair while the other finds her waist, she makes a soft sound that undoes me completely. She tastes like wine and promises, like every memory I've been trying to forget and every dream I've been afraid to have.

Her hands curl into my jacket, pulling me closer as the kiss deepens. Everything we've been fighting, everything we've been pretending not to feel, every careful boundary we've built - all of it falls away until there's just this.

Just us.

When we finally part, she stays close, her forehead resting against mine. Both of us breathing like we've run miles. Both of us knowing everything has changed again.

"So much for taking it slow." But her smile is radiant, even in the dim light.

"I'll still follow you home." My voice comes out rough. Hungry. "Make sure you're safe."

"Three cars back?" She traces my jaw with trembling fingers before stepping away.

"Always."

I watch her slide into her car, memorizing every detail of this moment. The way her hands shake slightly on the keys. The last lingering look she gives me before starting the engine. The promise of tomorrow in her smile.

That kiss has changed my life.

# *Beach Seduction*

## RAINE

**MY LIPS ARE STILL TINGLING** as I pull into my driveway. Will's headlights appear in my rearview, three cars back like always, but nothing about tonight feels routine. Nothing about that kiss in the parking lot was taking it slow.

I touch my mouth, remembering the way he tasted, the way his hands felt in my hair, against my waist. His body warm against mine. Professional distance seems like a dream now, something we were pretending at for far too long.

My phone buzzes as I unlock the door. Maya.

"Please tell me you're free for dinner Saturday." She doesn't bother with hello. "Devon's parents fly in Friday, and we need to do the whole family meal thing before the menu tasting."

Through the window, I watch Will's car idle at the corner. Waiting to make sure I'm safe, like always.

My skin still burns where he touched it, where his fingers traced my jaw before letting me go.

"Mom? Are you even listening?"

"Sorry, honey." I sink onto my couch, finally kicking off my heels. "What time Saturday?"

"Seven. Unless..." She pauses. "Unless you have plans. With, say, someone who took you to dinner?"

I close my eyes. "How did you—"

"You're not answering your phone on a Thursday night, you sound distracted, and Dad's car just went past Devon's place for like the third time."

*This neighborhood is too damned small.*

I touch my lips again without meaning to, remembering the look in Will's eyes under the streetlight. The way time disappeared when he kissed me.

"Mom?" Maya's voice sharpens. "What aren't you telling me?"

"Your father and I..." I pause, trying to find words for something that still feels like a dream. "Yes. We had dinner tonight."

Silence. Then: "Like, co-parent dinner? Wedding planning dinner?"

"No." I close my eyes. I can't believe I'm about to tell my daughter about our date. "Like a date. At Otium."

More silence. I can practically hear her processing this.

"Otium?" She sounds breathless suddenly. "That's... that's a *real* date. That's a trying-again date."

"We're taking it slow," I say, though my racing heart disagrees. Though I can still feel his hands in my hair, still taste him on my lips. "Being careful. Professional at work—"

"Oh my god." Now she's definitely not breathing. "Did he kiss you?"

The question catches me off guard. My silence must answer for me.

"He did!" She actually squeals. "Tell me everything. Now."

"Maya." I stand, needing to move. Needing to do something with this energy still coursing through me. "It's complicated."

"Was it good complicated?"

I pause at my window, where Will's headlights had been minutes ago. Remember how he tasted. How his hands shook slightly when he helped with my coat. How everything we've been trying to ignore crashed over us in that parking lot.

"Mom?"

"Yes." The admission comes softly. "It was... yes."

"I knew it." Her voice catches. "I knew you still... that he still..."

"We're trying to figure things out." I fidget with my bracelet, the one he gave me before Maya was born. "Slowly."

"Because of the tour? Lucas's new dates?"

"Because we don't want to mess this up." My

voice trembles slightly. "Not again. Not when it feels like..."

"Like what?"

"Like maybe we never really stopped." I can't stop the truth from coming out. "Like maybe we've just been pretending all these years."

"Mom." Her voice softens. "That's... that's exactly what we've all been seeing. You and Dad, you just... you make sense."

I sink back onto the couch, suddenly overwhelmed. By the kiss. By tonight. By my daughter's quiet certainty.

"We were supposed to take it slow," I whisper. "Be careful this time."

"And the kiss wasn't careful?"

"The kiss was..." I close my eyes, remembering. The jasmine in the air. The way his hand slid into my hair. How the world disappeared until there was just us. "Everything."

"So Saturday." Maya's tone turns practical, but I can hear her smile. "Devon's parents want to do dinner at this fancy place in Beverly Hills, but I was thinking somewhere more... us."

"Maya—"

"Just dinner. Family dinner. Like always." A pause. "Except maybe this time you and Dad won't have to pretend you're not stealing glances at each other across the table."

"We don't—"

"Mom. Please. Lucas and I have been watching you two dance around each other for years. At least now you're being honest about it."

My phone buzzes with a text.

WILL: Home safe?

"He's checking on you, isn't he?" Maya asks, knowing somehow. "Even after following you home?"

"Maybe." I type back quickly.

ME: Yes. Thank you for tonight.

His response comes immediately.

WILL: Thank you for the kiss.

"Mom? You still there?"

"Sorry." I bring the phone back to my ear, trying to focus. "About Saturday..."

"Have it there," she says softly. "In your new place. Let Dad help you cook, like he used to. Show Devon's parents who we really are."

I glance around my half-unpacked condo. At the kitchen I've barely touched except for coffee. At the life I'm slowly building. Or maybe rebuilding.

"Maya."

"What's the worst that could happen? You and

Dad end up in the kitchen together, remembering how good you are at this? At being us?"

Another text from Will.

WILL: Already missing you.

"Okay," I hear myself say. "Saturday. Here."

"Really?" She sounds like she did at five, when we'd give in to ice cream before dinner.

"Really." I look at Will's text, at the promise in those three words. "But we're taking it slow."

"Right." Her smile carries through the phone. "That kiss in the parking lot was definitely taking it slow."

"Maya Elizabeth."

"Love you, Mom." She pauses. "And Mom? I'm happy for you. For both of you."

After we hang up, I sit in the quiet of my condo, touching my lips again. Remembering. Feeling. Finally letting myself want.

My phone lights up one more time.

WILL: Sweet dreams, Raine.

# Lost In You

## WILL

**SHE ORDERED MY COFFEE AGAIN.** It's waiting at our usual table when I arrive, even though I'm early. Even though we're both pretending this is just our new morning routine and not an excuse to see each other before work.

"Professional enough for you?" Her eyes spark with amusement as I sit.

"Very." I resist the urge to touch her hand. To pull her close like last night. "Though you have something..."

She reaches for her lip automatically, and I catch the slight tremor in her fingers. Good to know I'm not the only one still thinking about that kiss.

"Just teasing." I grin as she rolls her eyes. "Sleep well?"

"You know I didn't." But her smile is warm. "Maya called right after I got home."

"Ah." I settle back, cradling my coffee. "So, she knows?"

"That we had dinner? Yes." She tucks her hair behind her ear - that nervous tell I've always loved. "That we kissed in the parking lot like teenagers? Also yes."

"Oh geez. And?"

"And she wants us to host Saturday's dinner with Devon's parents at my place."

I nearly choke on my coffee. "Your place? The one you've barely unpacked? And, more importantly, can you cook now?"

She ignores my obvious jab at her cooking skills. "The one with the great kitchen I never use." She traces the rim of her cup. "Maya thinks it would be more... us. Than some fancy Beverly Hills restaurant."

"Us." The word hangs between us, weighted with possibility. With last night's kiss and years of history.

"We don't have to—"

"I'll help you cook." The offer comes automatically. Like muscle memory. Like all the Sunday dinners we used to make together, Maya doing homework at the counter while Lucas banged on pots with wooden spoons.

"Will." Her voice softens. "That's not taking it slow."

"It's just dinner." But we both know it's not. Not after last night. Not with the way she's looking at me

118

now, like she's remembering the taste of my lips. The feel of my hands in her hair.

"Just dinner," she echoes. "With Devon's parents. And our kids. And..."

"And us." I reach for her hand finally, unable to help myself. "Whatever that means now."

Her fingers lace with mine like they never forgot how. Like years haven't passed since we first sat in a coffee shop, planning our future.

"Maya thinks we're inevitable," she says softly. "That we've just been pretending all these years."

"Smart kid." I run my thumb across her knuckles. "Gets it from her mother."

"Will." But she doesn't pull away. "What are we doing?"

"Right now? Having coffee." I squeeze her hand gently. "Tonight you have Netflix tracks to finish. I have drum parts to record. Saturday we'll cook dinner for our future in-laws."

"And the tour? Lucas's schedule? The album deadline?"

"We'll figure it out." I meet her eyes. "Together this time."

Her phone buzzes - probably the Netflix producers. Reality crashing back in.

"I should go." She starts gathering her things, but her hand lingers in mine. "Early session."

"Tonight?" The question slips out before I can stop it.

"Slow, remember?" But her smile holds promise. "One dinner at a time."

The control room feels empty without her, even though we've done plenty of sessions apart over the years. Even though we're supposed to be professionals.

"Earth to Will." Mark waves a hand in front of my face. "That fill in the bridge?"

"Sorry." I adjust my headphones. "One more pass."

"Man's distracted." Chase's voice carries that knowing tone. "Wouldn't have anything to do with a certain dinner at Otium last night?"

I miss a beat - *actually miss a beat*. Something I haven't done since we were kids playing dive bars.

"Knew it!" Chase kills the playback. "Spill. Now."

"There's nothing to—"

"Save it." Mark sets down his guitar. "We saw you two at coffee this morning. Holding hands is a new definition of 'professional discussion.' You might not want to sit right by the window."

"Fine." I pull off my headphones. No point pretending anymore. "We had dinner. We talked. We're... figuring things out."

"Figuring things out?" Chase snorts. "Is that what they call making out in parking lots now?"

My head snaps up. "How did you—"

Chase grins. "Maya texts me everything."

"Of course she does." I run a hand through my hair. "Look, it's new. We're taking it slow."

"Slow?" Mark laughs. "You've been in love with her for twenty-five years. The whole industry's been watching you two dance around each other since the divorce."

"It's different now." I fidget with my sticks. "We're different."

"Yeah." Chase's voice turns serious. "You are. Both of you. That's why it'll work this time."

"You sound pretty sure."

"Because I am." He settles into the control room chair - her chair. "Some of us know what it's like to waste years pretending you're not still in love with someone."

"This about you and Eliza?" Mark asks.

"This is about not being stupid anymore." Chase fixes me with a look. "About not letting fear stop you from having what you want. Speaking of what I want." Chase leans forward. "You're hosting dinner at her place Saturday?"

"How do you—"

"Maya," all three of us say together.

"Yes." I set my sticks down. "With Devon's parents. At her new place."

"The one you drive by every night?" Mark raises an eyebrow. "The one that just happens to be three blocks from yours?"

"The one she just happened to choose when Eric —" Chase starts.

"Can we work?" I cut him off. "Some of us have an album to finish."

"Sure." Chase's grin is insufferable. "Wouldn't want to keep you from your evening drive-by. Though maybe now you'll actually go inside instead of just checking the street."

"We're taking it slow," I repeat, but the words sound hollow even to me. Not after last night's kiss. Not with Saturday's dinner looming.

"Right." Mark picks up his guitar. "Slow. Professional. Just coffee."

"Just like me and Eliza were just casual." Chase's voice softens. "Until we weren't anymore."

I slip my headphones back on, trying to focus on the track. On anything except the memory of Raine's lips. The way she felt in my arms. The promise of Saturday night.

"From the bridge?" I ask, desperate to change the subject.

But Chase just smiles that knowing smile. "Whatever you say, drummer boy. Whatever you say."

# *Periscope*

## RAINE

MY KITCHEN HASN'T SEEN this much activity since... well, since Will and I used to host Sunday dinners. Now he's checking my knife work while dicing onions, close enough that I can feel his warmth against my back. Close enough that professional distance seems like a joke.

"Still rushing it." His hand covers mine on the knife, adjusting my grip. "Let the blade do the work."

I try to focus on the onions and not how his fingers feel against mine. Not how natural this is, him teaching me knife skills again like nothing's changed. Like we didn't spend years pretending we weren't still--

"You're still rushing." His voice holds that amused tone I remember from a thousand cooking lessons. From all the nights he tried to teach me patience in the kitchen. "Some things never change."

"Says the man who probably still can't fold a fitted sheet." I twist to look at him, forgetting how close he's standing. His eyes catch mine, and suddenly I'm remembering that kiss in the parking lot. The way time disappeared when his lips met mine.

"That's what I kept you around for." His smile is soft, dangerous. "Among other things."

"Is that so?" I arch an eyebrow, trying to ignore how my heart speeds up when his hand slides to my waist. "I seem to remember you being the one who couldn't resist my coffee."

"Your coffee?" He laughs, the sound rumbling through me where we touch. "You mean the coffee you still order exactly how I like it? Every morning?"

"Professional courtesy." But we both know it's more. Have always known, even when we were pretending otherwise.

"Very professional." His fingers trace small circles on my hip, and I forget what I was chopping. What I was saying. Why we ever thought we could keep this slow. "And I still hate that word."

"Will." His name comes out breathier than I meant it to.

"Hmm?" His lips brush my temple, and suddenly we're swaying slightly, like we're dancing to music only we can hear. Like we're twenty-three again, learning to cook together in our first apartment.

"The onions," I manage, but I make no move to step away.

"They can wait." He turns me slowly, until I'm facing him. Until there's nothing between us but years of memories and moments like this. "I've waited long enough."

When he kisses me, it tastes like coming home. Like Sunday dinners and morning coffee and every moment we tried to pretend we weren't still in love. His hands slide into my hair, and I forget about Devon's parents, about taking it slow, about everything except how right this feels.

"I missed this," he murmurs against my lips. "Missed us."

"Even my terrible knife skills?" I smile into the kiss, feeling his laugh vibrate through me.

"Especially those." He pulls back just enough to meet my eyes. "They gave me an excuse to stand this close."

"You never needed an excuse." The truth is heavy between us.

His expression softens. "No. I didn't. I just needed the courage to do something about it."

My phone buzzes, breaking the moment.

> MAYA: On our way with Devon's parents. They wanted to see the sunset from Griffith Observatory first.

"They're running late." I try to steady my voice, to

ignore how his hands feel on my waist. "Maya's showing them the Observatory."

"Good." Will steps away and tastes the sauce, then reaches past me for the herbs. His arm brushes mine deliberately this time, playful. "Gives me more time to critique your technique."

"My technique?" I steal a taste of sauce from his spoon, watching his eyes darken. "I seem to remember you being quite fond of my... technique."

"Careful." He sets down the spoon, backing me against the counter. "Or we'll never get dinner ready."

"Would that be so terrible?" I loop my arms around his neck, feeling reckless. Happy. "Maya did say to show them who we really are."

"And who are we?" The question holds weight this time, possibility.

I kiss him softly, tasting herbs and promise. "We're figuring that out."

"Together?" His forehead rests against mine.

"Together."

My phone buzzes again.

> MAYA: Please tell me dinner's actually cooking and you and Dad aren't just making eyes at each other.

Will reads over my shoulder, laughing. "Should we tell her we're being completely professional?"

"Absolutely." I try to step away, but he pulls me

back for one more kiss. Quick but full of promise. "Just cooking."

"Just cooking," he agrees, but his eyes say something else. Like parking lot kisses and Sunday dinners and twenty-five years of knowing exactly how we move together in a kitchen.

The timer dings, and he reluctantly lets me go. I straighten my apron, trying to remember we're hosting Devon's parents. That this isn't just another dinner, another chance to fall in love all over again.

"Your hair." He reaches out, tucking a strand behind my ear. His fingers linger on my cheek. "Dead giveaway."

"Says the man with sauce on his collar." I fix his shirt, letting my hands rest on his chest longer than necessary. "What happened to taking it slow?"

"We did slow." He captures my hand, pressing a kiss to my palm. "For twenty years. Think that's slow enough?"

Another text.

> MAYA: Ten minutes out. You two better be decent.

"We should probably actually cook something." I laugh, but I don't move away. Can't move away, not when he's looking at me like that. Like no time has passed at all.

"Probably." He steals one more kiss before turning

127

back to the stove. "But for the record? I like this version of us better."

"Which version is that?"

His smile holds Sunday dinners and morning coffee and every moment we've been pretending we weren't still in love. "The honest one."

The sauce bubbles, reminding us we have actual dinner to prepare. Real guests coming. A family to host.

"Will?" I hand him the herbs he's reaching for, loving how our fingers brush. How natural this feels.

"Hmm?"

"I like this version too."

His smile is everything. "Good. Because your knife work still needs practice."

"Maybe I need more lessons."

His eyes darken with promise. "Careful what you wish for."

## WILL

DEVON'S MOTHER is studying the photos on Raine's mantel, and I can't help wondering if she notices how many of them include me. How many moments we've shared, even after everything. Even when we were pretending we could be just co-parents, just colleagues, just anything except what we've always been.

"You've played Madison Square Garden?" She peers at a shot of Incendiary Ink from our last tour. "Multiple times?"

"Mom," Devon starts, but she's already moved on to the next photo. Maya and Lucas at the Grammys last year, Raine accepting her Producer of the Year award the year before, me teaching Lucas drums when his feet couldn't reach the pedals.

"It's just..." She glances between Raine and me, clearly recalibrating her expectations of her future in-laws. "Devon said you were in the music industry, but..."

"Dad's band is kind of a big deal," Maya says from the kitchen, where she's helping Raine with dessert. "And Mom's produced like half the voices you hear on the radio."

I watch Raine duck her head at the praise, that familiar mix of pride and modesty I've always loved. She catches my eye across the room and smiles – that private smile that's been making my heart stop for twenty-five years.

*"The dessert,"* she mouths, and I know she needs a moment. Needs me to run interference while she steadies herself.

"Actually," I stand, moving toward the kitchen, "let me tell you about the time Lucas decided to redesign my drum kit. He was four, had gotten into Raine's nail polish..."

Devon's father laughs – the first real laugh we've gotten from him all night. "Devon went through a similar phase. Though it was my law books he decided needed decorating."

"That's right," I remember something Maya mentioned. "You teach at Harvard Law?"

"Constitutional law." He straightens slightly. "Though I understand Maya's chosen corporate law?"

"Best decision I ever made." Maya appears with the dessert plates. "Well, that and saying yes to Devon."

"Speaking of decisions." Devon's mother has found the wedding photo. The one of Raine and me that I'm surprised she keeps displayed. "You two were so young."

"Mom." Devon's warning is clearer this time.

"We were," Raine says, returning with dessert. Her hand brushes my arm as she passes – deliberate, steadying. "But some things you just know."

The loaded silence that follows is broken by Lucas arriving late, apologizing about traffic from rehearsal. He hugs his mother, does that handshake-half-hug thing with me, then freezes when he sees the tableau around the wedding photo.

"Oh." He glances between us, reading the room. "Are we doing the story about the nail polish? Because I maintain that drum kit looked better with glitter."

Just like that, the tension breaks. Devon's father asks about Lucas's band, which leads to a discussion about vintage guitars, which somehow ends with plans to visit Devon's collection.

I watch it all from the kitchen, where I'm helping Raine with coffee. Where I can stand close enough to smell her perfume, to feel the warmth of her beside me.

"They're going to be fine," I murmur, low enough that only she can hear.

"I know." She leans into me slightly, either forgetting or not caring that Maya can probably see us. "I just want..."

"Everything to be perfect?" I risk touching her waist, hidden by the counter. "Some things never change."

She turns, ready to argue, but something in my expression stops her. Makes her eyes darken with memories of earlier, of kisses that tasted like sauce and possibility.

"The coffee," she says softly, but she doesn't move away.

"Let it steep." I trace small circles on her hip, watching her breath catch. "Some things are worth waiting for."

"Will." My name holds warning, but her hand comes to rest on my chest.

"I know." I force myself to step back, to remember we have an audience. To ignore how right this feels, us in the kitchen together, making coffee like we used to. "Professional," I tease in a sing-song voice.

Her laugh is shaky. "Not even close."

Maya catches me watching Raine as she walks Devon's parents to their car. Even in the dark, I can read my daughter's knowing smile.

"You're staying, right?" She gathers dessert plates with practiced efficiency. "To help clean up?"

"Maya." I try for stern but probably miss by miles. "We're taking--"

"Taking it slow. Right." She stacks cups with more force than necessary. "Because that's totally what was happening in the kitchen earlier."

"You saw that?"

Her eye roll is pure Raine. "Dad. Everyone saw that. Devon's mom was practically taking notes."

Before I can respond, Lucas appears with the wine glasses. "Speaking of notes, I have some thoughts about the new tour schedule."

"Now?" I start loading the dishwasher, needing something to do with my hands. Needing not to think about how Raine felt pressed against me in the kitchen.

"Better now than tomorrow when you're..." He waves vaguely. "Distracted."

"I don't get distracted." But even I can hear the lie in my voice.

"Sure." Maya hands me another stack of plates. "That's why you missed a fill during recording yesterday. For the first time since, what, 1999?"

"You told her about that?" I glare at Lucas.

"Chase told her." He grins. "Something about being too busy thinking about dinner at Otium?"

"Don't you two have somewhere to be?" I try for authoritative father but probably land closer to desperately seeking privacy.

"Actually..." Maya draws out the word. "Devon's taking his parents back to their hotel, and I have that brief to finish..."

"And I should really get some sleep before tomorrow's session..." Lucas backs toward the door with exaggerated casualness.

"Tomorrow is Sunday…"

He reddens and shrugs with a smirk.

"Subtle." I shake my head. "Really subtle."

"We learned from the best." Maya kisses my cheek. "Love you, Dad. Try not to mess this up."

"Thanks for the vote of confidence."

"Oh, we're confident." Lucas comes back and hugs me quickly. "Just also..."

"Invested?" Maya supplies.

"Invested." He nods. "That's a good word for it."

They're still plotting as they leave, heads bent together like when they were kids planning how to stay up past bedtime. I hear Maya's laugh, then the door closing, then...silence.

Raine appears in the kitchen doorway, backlit by the living room light. For a moment, I'm thrown back twenty-odd years – her in our old kitchen, wearing my shirt, smiling that smile that's only ever been mine.

"They're plotting." She moves to the sink, close enough that I can smell her perfume. "Again."

"They're good at it." I hand her a pan to dry. "Wonder where they get that from?"

"Definitely you." She bumps my hip with hers. "I seem to remember someone plotting quite a few things back in the day."

"Like accidentally booking studio time that over-lapped with your sessions?"

"Or mysteriously being at every showcase I produced?"

"Pure coincidence." But we're both smiling now, remembering. "Industry's not that big."

"Right." She sets down the dish towel, turning to face me, her eyes sparkling.

"And you just happened to buy a house three blocks from my place?" I smirk, knowing I've caught her.

"Good school district," she says innocently as I step closer, drawn by the light in her eyes. By the memory of how she tasted earlier.

"The kids are grown."

Her hands come to rest on my chest. "Good restaurants?"

"You hate eating out alone."

"Fine." But she's smiling as she says it.

I cup her face, loving how she leans into my touch. "I missed you. Every day. Even when I was pretending I didn't."

"Will." My name holds decades of history. Of moments like this.

"I know." I brush my thumb across her cheek. "Slow. Professional. Just helping with dishes."

She laughs softly. "I think we're past professional."

"Past slow, too," I murmur, closing the distance between us.

This kiss is different from earlier. Slower. Deeper. Like we have all the time in the world to remember how we fit together. How we've always fit together.

"Stay," she whispers against my lips, and my heart stops.

Some decisions make themselves.

## Spell On Me

### RAINE

**WILL'S** hands shake slightly as he undoes my buttons, like he's twenty-three again and we're still learning each other. Like we haven't done this a thousand times before. His touch is familiar and new all at once – the calluses from his sticks, the gentle way he traces my collarbone, the heat in his eyes when he looks at me.

"You're sure?" he whispers against my neck, and I hear the vulnerability beneath the desire. The fear that this could shatter everything we're rebuilding.

"I've never been more sure." I thread my fingers through his hair, drawing him up to kiss me properly. "Have you?"

His answer is in the way he kisses me – deep and thorough and full of twenty-five years of knowing exactly how to make me gasp. His hands slide under my shirt, finding all the places that make me arch against him, and suddenly we're both trembling.

"God, I've missed you," he breathes against my skin. "Every day. Even when I was pretending I didn't."

I pull back just enough to meet his eyes, to let him see everything I've been hiding. "I missed you too. Even when I was with..."

"Don't." He presses his forehead to mine. "We're here now. That's what matters."

My hands find the buttons of his shirt, remembering how this goes. How we've always gone together, like rhythm and melody, like drums and voice. His breath catches when I trace the tattoo over his heart – the one he got when Maya was born, her name in my handwriting.

"You kept it." My voice catches. It's stupid to say, but the sight of it after all this time throws me.

"Of course I did." He kisses me softly with a light laugh. "Tattoos are kinda permanent."

The word *'permanent'* hangs between us, weighted with possibility. With everything we're risking by doing this again. Everything we could lose if we get it wrong.

But then his hands slide lower, and thought becomes impossible. Memory becomes irrelevant. There's only this – us, together, finding our rhythm again like we never lost it.

His lips trace a familiar path down my neck, and

memories flood back – our first apartment, early mornings before the kids woke up, stolen moments in recording studios. But this is different too. Slower. More certain. Like we finally understand what we have to lose, what we have to gain.

"Will." His name catches in my throat as his hands find bare skin. "I need..."

"I know." He draws back to look at me, and the love in his eyes nearly breaks me. "I've always known."

The rest of our clothes fall away with practiced ease, muscle memory taking over where conscious thought fails. His hands remember every curve, every sensitive spot, every way to make me gasp his name. My fingers find the places that make him groan – the spot behind his ear, the hollow of his hip, the sensitive skin along his spine.

"How did we ever think we could be just friends?" I whisper as he lowers me to the bed. "Just colleagues?"

He laughs against my skin. "We were never very good at it."

"No." I arch as his mouth finds my breast. "We really weren't."

Time blurs then, measured only in touches and tastes and shared breaths. In the way he still knows exactly how to touch me, how to build the tension until I'm trembling beneath him. In how perfectly we still fit together, like puzzle pieces finally clicking into place.

"Look at me," he murmurs as he enters me, and I do. See everything I'm feeling reflected in his eyes – love, desire, hope, fear. The certainty that this is right, has always been right.

"I love you." The words slip out without conscious thought, but they feel as natural as breathing. As inevitable as the rhythm building between us.

His movements falter, and for a moment I'm afraid I've said too much too soon. But then he kisses me deeply, desperately, like he's trying to pour thirteen years of unspoken feelings into a single kiss.

"I never stopped," he breathes against my lips. "Not for a single day."

The confession breaks something loose in both of us. Suddenly we're moving faster, harder, need overwhelming the desire to take things slow. His hands find mine, pinning them above my head as he drives deeper, and I'm lost in sensation. In memory. In the perfect rightness of us together.

When I come apart beneath him, it feels like coming home.

After, he traces lazy patterns on my skin while I listen to his heartbeat slow. The familiar weight of his arm around me, the way my head fits perfectly in the crook of his shoulder – it's like the past dissolves, leaving only this.

*Only us.*

"Your hair's different," he murmurs, running his fingers through the silver strands I've stopped coloring. "I like it."

"Liar." But I smile against his chest. "You just like that you can still find all my weak spots."

"Those haven't changed." His hand slides to my hip, thumb brushing the sensitive place that always makes me shiver. "Neither has the way you say my name when you..."

"Will." I nip his shoulder lightly.

"Exactly like that." His laugh rumbles through me, and suddenly I'm fighting tears. "Hey." He tilts my chin up. "What's wrong?"

"Nothing." I blink hard. "Everything. I just... I forgot how this felt. How we felt. And now..."

"Now we're here." He kisses me softly. Kisses away my tears. "Together. Finally being honest about what we want."

"Are we crazy?" I prop myself up to look at him properly. "Trying this again? With the tour coming up, and Lucas's schedule, and Maya's wedding..."

"Probably." His hands slide into my hair, drawing me down for another kiss. "But we tried being sensible. Being professional. How'd that work out?"

"Terrible." I smile against his lips. "We were awful at it."

"The worst." He rolls us suddenly, pinning me beneath him. "Remember that session at Capitol? When you were producing Chase's vocals?"

"When you kept missing fills because I bent over the console?"

"In that red dress." His eyes darken at the memory. "Mark had to hit me with a stick to get my attention."

"I wore it on purpose." The confession slips out easily now. "I knew you'd be there."

"Tease." But he's smiling as he kisses down my neck. "What about the Grammy party? When you kept touching my arm while talking to that Netflix executive?"

"You were tapping rhythms on my back the whole time." I gasp as his mouth finds my breast. "Very unprofessional."

"We were terrible at professional." His hand slides between my legs, making thought impossible. "Awful at casual."

"The worst at... oh God, there..."

Words become irrelevant then, lost in the rediscovery of us. In the perfect way he remembers how to touch me, how to move with me, how to make me forget everything except this. Him. Us.

After the second time – or maybe the third, I've lost count – we lie tangled in sheets and memories, his fingers tracing my spine while I draw idle patterns on his chest.

"Stay," I whisper, though it's well past midnight.

"Try to make me leave." He kisses my temple, my

cheek, my lips. "I'm done pretending I don't want to be exactly where I am."

"Even with everything coming up? The tour, the album deadline..."

"Especially with all that." His arms tighten around me. "I'm tired of missing you when you're right there. Of trying to keep things professional when all I want..."

"What?" I prop myself up to see his face. "What do you want?"

His smile is everything I remember. Everything I've missed. Everything I want for the rest of my life.

"This. Us. Always."

Simple words. But they hold twenty-five years of history. Of love and loss and finding our way back. Of finally being exactly where we belong.

I kiss him deeply, putting everything I can't say into it. All the years of wanting, of pretending, of trying to be anything except what we've always been.

"Always," I agree, and feel his smile against my lips.

*Always.*

# Follow You

## WILL

RAINE'S still asleep when I wake, curled against me like no time has passed. Like we're still those kids in our first apartment, with nothing but dreams and demo tapes and absolute certainty that we belonged together.

We spent all of Sunday like this, but at my house this time. Staying in bed, rediscovering each other, eating takeout from cartons, and then more…

Her hair spills across my chest, silver strands catching the early morning light. New and familiar all at once, like everything about us now. I trace my fingers along her spine, memorizing this moment. The weight of her against me. The quiet rhythm of her breathing. The way she still fits perfectly in my arms.

"Watching me sleep?" she murmurs without opening her eyes. "Some things never change."

"Can't help it." I press a kiss to her temple. "You're still the most beautiful thing I've ever seen."

"Smooth talker." But she snuggles closer, pressing a sleepy kiss to my chest. Right over the tattoo of Maya's name. "What time is it?"

"Early." I glance at her bedside clock – 5:47. "Though if we want coffee before your Netflix session..."

"Don't remind me." She groans, but makes no move to get up. "I have to be professional in three hours."

"Very professional," I say. The word now a private joke between us. I let my hand slide lower, loving how she arches into my touch. "Absolutely focused on work."

"Will." My name holds warning, but her leg hooks over mine. "We don't have time..."

"We always have time." I roll her beneath me, drinking in her sleep-warm smile. "Some things are worth being late for."

"Is that so?" Her hands thread through my hair as I kiss down her neck. "And what will you tell the band?"

"That their producer kept me up late discussing..." I nip her collarbone lightly. "Technical details."

Her laugh turns to a gasp as my hands find a sensitive spot. "Very technical."

"Extremely." I trace the familiar path down her

body, remembering every inch that makes her breath catch. "Could take hours to properly... review."

"Hours?" But she's already moving with me, against me, like we never forgot this dance. "What happened to taking it slow?"

I lift my head to meet her eyes, suddenly serious. "I think we're way past that, don't you?"

Her expression softens. "Way past it."

Then her hand slides between us, and talking becomes irrelevant. There's only sensation – the taste of her skin, the sound of my name on her lips, the perfect rhythm we find together. Like muscle memory.

Like finally admitting what we've known all along.

After, we share a shower – "to save time," we tell ourselves, though we both know better. She uses my shoulder for balance as she washes her hair, and I'm thrown back to a thousand mornings like this. To early recording sessions and rushed breakfasts and kids banging on the bathroom door.

"You're thinking too loud," she says, catching my expression in the steamy mirror as she does her makeup. She's wearing my shirt, and the sight does things to my heart I can't quite explain.

"Just remembering." I wrap my arms around her from behind, pressing a kiss to her shoulder. "How many times we've done this."

"The shower part or the being late to session

part?" But her smile in the mirror is soft. Understanding.

"All of it." I rest my chin on her head, watching her put on mascara with practiced precision. "Though I distinctly remember you having more clothes back then."

"You offering to clear me some drawer space, Knightly?" She tries for teasing, but I hear the question underneath.

"Maybe." I meet her eyes in the mirror. "Though it seems a waste when I live three blocks away."

Her hand stills on her lipstick. "Will..."

"I'm just saying." I kiss her temple, careful not to disrupt her makeup routine. "Seems silly to keep pretending we're taking it slow. That this isn't exactly where we want to be."

She turns in my arms, expression serious. "The tour starts in three weeks."

"I know."

"Lucas has those new dates with Another Angel."

"I know that too."

"The album deadline..."

"Raine." I cup her face, thumbs brushing her cheekbones. "I know all of it. And I don't care. I'm done missing you when you're right there. Done pretending I don't want to wake up with you every morning."

"Even with everything coming up?" But her hands

are sliding up my chest, contradicting her practical tone.

"Especially with everything coming up." I kiss her softly, tasting coffee and toothpaste and possibility. "I want this. Us. All of it."

"The industry will talk." But she's smiling now, that smile that's only ever been mine.

"Let them." I pull her closer, not caring that we're making ourselves later by the minute. "They've been talking for years anyway. At least now they'll be right."

Her laugh vibrates through me. "Chase is going to be insufferable."

"Chase has been insufferable since 1999." I steal another kiss, longer this time. "And Maya's going to say she told us so."

"Lucas too." She starts fixing my collar, a gesture so familiar it makes my throat tight. "They've been plotting this for months."

"Years," I correct, catching her hands. "Remember that 'accidental' double booking at the studio last Christmas?"

"Or the way they kept mentioning how close my new place was to yours?"

"Very subtle, our children."

"They get that from you." She reaches for her lipstick again, but I catch her wrist.

"Leave it."

Her eyebrow arches. "I have a session in forty minutes."

"Exactly." I back her against the counter, loving how her breath catches. "Plenty of time."

"Will." But she's already tilting her head back, already sliding her hands into my hair. "We're going to be so late."

"Worth it." I trail kisses down her neck, carefully avoiding her freshly applied makeup. "Some things are more important than being on time."

"Like what?" But her leg is hooking around mine, pulling me closer.

"Like making sure..." I unbutton the shirt she's wearing – my shirt – with deliberate slowness. "That you remember exactly why being professional is overrated."

"Traffic must have been terrible this morning." Chase looks pointedly at the coffee cups in our hands. "Since you clearly didn't have time to stop for your usual..."

"Can we work?" I try for professional, but probably miss by miles. Especially with the way Raine's fighting a smile beside me.

"Sure." Chase settles into the control room chair.

"Though you might want to..." He gestures vaguely at his neck.

Raine's eyes widen, and she hurries to the bathroom. When she returns, her cheeks are pink, but her eyes meet mine with a mix of embarrassment and something else. Something that tastes like twenty-five years of knowing exactly how we fit together.

"If we could focus on the bridge," she says, all business now despite the color in her cheeks. "The fill needs..."

"Absolutely." I adjust my headphones, trying not to watch her slide into her producer chair. Trying not to remember how she felt in my arms an hour ago. "From the top?"

But Chase is texting someone, grinning. "Maya says it's about damn time."

"Chase." Raine's warning tone would be more effective if she wasn't smiling.

"What? We've all been watching you two dance around each other for years." He sets his phone down. "Though I gotta say, hickeys are a new level of unprofessional..."

"The bridge?" I cut in, but I can't help smiling too. Can't help catching Raine's eye through the glass, seeing everything I'm feeling reflected back.

We actually do work then, falling into the familiar rhythm of session and playback. But everything's different now. The way she speaks into my headphones, low and intimate like she used to. The casual touches as she adjusts my monitor mix. The loaded glances that hold promises for later.

Mark arrives halfway through, takes one look at us, and just says, "Finally."

I should be embarrassed by how obvious we are. Should care about maintaining some semblance of professionalism. But all I can think about is how right this feels. How natural. Like we're finally done pretending this isn't exactly where we belong.

"One more pass," Raine says into my headphones, and her voice holds everything. Memory and promise. Past and future. The certainty that we're done wasting time.

My phone buzzes with a text.

> LUCAS: Mom's wearing your shirt.
> Subtle.

Then another.

> LUCAS: Also, you owe me $50. I
> TOLD you she'd make the first
> move.

I look up to find Raine watching me, that private smile playing at her lips. The one that's only ever been mine. The one that says everything we don't need words for anymore.

Chase starts the playback, and I close my eyes, letting the music wash over me. Letting myself feel the perfect rightness of this moment. Of us. Of finally being exactly where we're meant to be.

"Ready?" Raine's voice in my headphones is everything I've ever wanted.

More than ready.

The fill flows perfectly this time, like it was always meant to. Like we were always meant to find our way back here. Back to us.

When I open my eyes, she's smiling that smile again. The one that says we're done pretending. Done being professional. Done being anything except what we've always been.

Together.

Finally.

# Choke

RAINE

**THREE WEEKS FEELS** like nothing and forever all at once. Like we've barely had time to find our rhythm again before everything changes. Will's bag sits by my door – *our* door, really, since he's been here almost every other night since that first night. Since we stopped pretending we were taking it slow.

"You're thinking too loud." His arms slide around me from behind as I stare at the tour schedule pinned to my fridge. Three months of dates and cities for the East Coast leg, with Another Angel opening for Incendiary Ink. Except for Cleveland – the first time Lucas's band branches out on their own while Incendiary Ink goes to Pittsburgh for press.

"Just memorizing." I trace the conflicting dates with my finger. "Making sure I know where you'll both be."

"We'll call." He presses a kiss to my neck. "Every

night. And you'll be out for the New York shows next month anyway."

"I know." But my hand trembles slightly as I touch the schedule. As I remember other tours, other goodbyes. The way distance used to crack us apart so slowly we didn't notice until it was too late.

"Hey." He turns me to face him, thumb brushing my cheek. "This isn't like before."

"No?" But I lean into his touch, needing his certainty. "Because it feels pretty familiar. The bus call, the schedule, the promises to call..."

"The incredibly hot producer wearing my shirt?" His smile is gentle. "The one I'm actually going to call this time, because I'm done pretending I don't need to hear her voice every day?"

"Will." But I'm smiling now too, despite the ache in my chest.

"I mean it." He pulls me closer, until I can feel his heartbeat against mine. "We're different now. Older. Smarter."

"Done pretending?"

"Done pretending." He kisses me softly. "Done running. Done letting distance be an excuse."

I close my eyes, remembering how young we were that third tour. How sure we were that love would be enough. That nothing could touch us as long as we had each other.

"I was so angry," I whisper against his chest.

"When you'd miss calls. When weeks would go by with just texts and voicemails..."

"I know." His arms tighten around me. "I was terrible at it. At balancing everything. At making you feel like a priority even when I was gone."

"We both were." I look up at him, needing him to understand. "I threw myself into producing, into proving I could do it all. Being the perfect mom, the rising star producer..."

"The one who never needed anyone." His smile is sad now. "Until we forgot how to need each other at all."

"But Cleveland..." My voice catches. "Will, it's his first show without you there. His first time really on his own, and his diabetes..."

"Mark's already arranged to have someone drive him there, while we're in Pittsburgh." His promise is fierce. "And I've talked to their tour manager about his schedule, his monitoring routine. They know what to watch for."

"Even with the separate dates?"

"Especially then." He cups my face, thumbs brushing away tears I didn't realize were falling. "He's not alone out there. I promise."

"I know." And I do. Will's always been the steady one, the protector. The one who checks streetlights and drives by at night and makes sure everyone's safe. "I just..."

"Worry?" His smile is tender. "That's what you do. It's one of the things I love about you."

The word catches me off guard, even though he's been saying it freely since that first night. Like we've both finally stopped being afraid of what we feel, of what we've always felt.

"We have a plan this time," he continues, fingers trailing down my spine. "Real plan, not just good intentions. Daily FaceTime, not just calls. Actual scheduled time, not just 'when we can.'"

"Between shows and sound checks and meet-and-greets?" But I'm smiling now, remembering how he programmed his phone to remind him. How he made me do the same.

"Every night at eleven, your time." He kisses my temple. "Even if it's just five minutes from the bus. Even if I'm half asleep or you're still in the studio."

"And the weekend visits?" I trace the collar of his shirt – my favorite of his shirts, really, the soft black one that smells like him.

"Opening night at the Garden, with Maya." His certainty steadies me. "Then, Philly for Lucas's birthday..."

"Will." My heart clenches with how much I love him. How much I've always loved him, even when I was pretending I didn't. But Lucas...

He instantly knows where my thoughts went. As always.

"He's our son." His voice roughens. "And yeah,

he's grown, and yeah, he manages his health well, but... he's our boy. But, don't worry. Mark will be there. *I* needed to know someone would be there."

"Mark's good with his routines," I acknowledge, a lump still in my throat. "He's known Lucas's schedule since..."

"Since he was diagnosed." Will's arms tighten around me. "He was the one who caught the signs that first time, remember? At rehearsal?"

"I remember." Of course I remember. The fear, the hospital, the way Mark had noticed Lucas's excessive thirst and fatigue before anyone else. "He's always looked out for him."

"For all of us." Will's smile is soft. "He's the one who kept telling me I was an idiot for letting you go."

"Us." The word is like sweet candy on my tongue.

"Always us." He kisses me deeply, thoroughly, until I forget about tours and schedules and everything except how right this feels. "There's no me without you anymore. Hasn't been for thirteen years, even when I was pretending otherwise."

"Even when I was with Eric?" I need to know. Need to hear it.

"Even then." His hands slide under my shirt – his shirt – finding bare skin. "I used to drive by his place too. Making sure you were safe."

"You didn't."

"Almost every night." His smile is sheepish now.

"Ask Maya. She used to track my phone, worried I was being crazy."

"You *were* being crazy." But I pull him closer, needing his warmth. His steadiness. "*Are* being crazy, with all these plans."

"Crazy about you." He nips my ear lightly. "Always have been."

"Smooth talker." But we're swaying now, like we're dancing to that same music only we can hear.

"Truth talker." His hands span my waist, and memories flood back – first dances and quiet kitchens and every moment we've moved together like this. "I'm done pretending I don't need you. Done acting like I can do any of this without you with me, even if you're just on my phone screen."

His phone buzzes – the first bus call warning. One hour until they leave for the Garden, for three months of stages and cities and missing each other.

"Don't." He catches my expression. "We've got time."

"An hour." But I let him pull me closer, let myself breathe in his scent. The one I'll be missing on his pillow.

"Exactly." His hands slide lower, deliberate now. "Plenty of time to remind you why you fell in love with me in the first place."

"Your modesty?" But I'm already arching into his touch, already forgetting about schedules and tours and everything except how he makes me feel.

"My timing." He backs me toward the bedroom – our bedroom now, really. "My attention to detail..."

"Your way with words?" I laugh against his lips as we tumble onto the bed.

"Among other things." His smile holds promise as he settles over me. "Let me show you."

Time slows then, measured only in touches and tastes and whispered promises. In the way he makes me forget everything except us, together, finding our rhythm like we never lost it.

After, I trace the familiar planes of his chest while he plays with my hair. Memorizing. Remembering.

"I'll see you in three days." His voice is soft in the dim light. "Opening night at the Garden."

"With Maya." I press a kiss over his heart, where our daughter's name is inked in my handwriting. "Front row, watching both our boys own that stage."

"Both of them." Pride and worry mix in his voice. "Lucas is ready, you know. For Cleveland. For all of it."

"I know." And I do. Our son is stronger than my fears, more capable than my worries. "Just promise me..."

"Mark will be there." He tilts my chin up. "The whole show. And Chase made sure their manager knows all Lucas's routines, his schedule..."

"And you'll call." It's not a question, but he answers anyway.

"Every night at eleven." He kisses me deeply. "Your time. No matter what."

His phone buzzes again. Thirty minutes.

"I should shower." But he makes no move to let me go.

"Probably." I trace the familiar pattern of calluses on his fingers, memorizing. "Since you smell like..."

"You?" His smile is wicked now. "Good. Gives me something to remember until Boston."

"Will." But I'm smiling too, even as my heart aches with how much I'll miss him.

"I love you." He says it easily now, like breathing. Like truth. "Every day, every city, every stage. No matter how far apart we are."

"Even when I'm being crazy and calling about Lucas's readings?"

"Especially then." He kisses me softly. "Because you're you, and I'm me, and we're finally done pretending that's not exactly how we want it."

The next buzz of his phone makes us both sigh. Twenty minutes.

"Shower." I push at his chest halfheartedly. "You smell like sex and promises."

"Good promises?" He steals one more kiss before rolling away.

"The best ones." I watch him head for the bathroom, memorizing this too. The way he looks in my room, in our life, in every moment we're done wasting. "The ones we're finally ready to keep."

# Fade In/Fade Out

~⌒~

## SEVEN WEEKS LATER
### WILL

**THE BUSES ARE HEADING** in opposite directions when I finally get Lucas on FaceTime. He's clearly just woken up, hair sticking up exactly like mine used to at his age. Like it still does, if I'm honest.

"Dad." He stifles a yawn. "I was just about to check in."

"With your readings?" I try to keep my tone casual. "Because Mark mentioned yesterday—"

"That I was a little low after soundcheck?" His eye roll is pure Raine. "I had a juice. I'm fine."

"A juice isn't really—"

"Dad." There's that tone I've been hearing more lately. Patient but firm. Adult. "I've been managing this since I was twelve. I know what I'm doing."

I bite back the urge to remind him about last week's incident in North Carolina. About how the heat and the endless meet-and-greets had sent his sugar crashing right before the show.

"I know you do." I adjust my phone, watching the Pennsylvania landscape blur past. "Just making sure you're taking care of yourself with the schedule change. First time without the regular opener slot..."

"Which is awesome." His whole face lights up, and suddenly he's my little boy again, excited about his first real drum kit. "You should see the production they're letting us use. Full lights, proper sound check, not just the quick line check we get with you guys..."

"That's great, but—"

"And the venue's social media team wants to do this whole thing about drummer legacies." He's not even listening now, caught up in the excitement. "They found these old shots of you playing Cleveland back in the day."

"Lucas." I hate interrupting his enthusiasm, but I need to know. "What are your numbers?"

The slight pause tells me everything.

"Haven't checked yet." He's not meeting my eyes now. "Just woke up."

"Lucas."

"I will." That tone again. The one that says he's humoring me. "Right after this call. Promise."

"And you'll text them to me?"

Now the eye roll comes with a sigh. "Dad. Seriously. I'm fine. The tour's going great, the band's killing it, and I haven't had any real issues—"

"Charlotte wasn't a real issue?"

"Charlotte was a combination of factors that I handled." His jaw sets in that way that means he's done discussing it. "I appreciate everyone's concern, but I've got this."

I study his face through the small screen. The shadows under his eyes from too many late nights. The slight tremor in his hand as he pushes his hair back.

"You're sure Mark doesn't need to—"

"I'm sure." His voice softens slightly. "Really, Dad. I know my limits. I know my body. And I know you and Mom are worried, but I'm not a kid anymore."

"No." My throat tightens unexpectedly. "You're not."

A voice calls something in the background – probably their tour manager.

"I gotta go." Lucas glances over his shoulder. "Production meeting about tonight's setup."

"Text me your numbers?" I hate how it comes out like a question.

"As soon as I check." He manages a smile. "Love you, Dad. Tell Mom I'll call her after the show."

"Lucas—"

But he's already gone, leaving me staring at a dark screen and trying to ignore the knot in my stomach.

My phone buzzes with a text from Mark.

> MARK: Made sure his kit's stocked with juice and protein bars. Got his backup monitor in my bag.

Then another.

> MARK: He'll be fine, man. Stop worrying.

But that's the thing about being a parent. You never really stop worrying.

Especially when you can see the crash coming.

I hit Raine's number before I can stop myself, needing to hear her voice. Needing to share this gnawing worry with the only other person who really understands.

"He's not checking his readings, is he?" She doesn't bother with hello.

"Says he was about to." I watch signs for Pittsburgh flash past. "Right after running off to a production meeting."

"Without eating breakfast." The worry in her voice mirrors mine. "Will, the last three shows—"

"I know." I close my eyes, remembering how pale he looked in Charlotte. How his hands shook during the meet-and-greet in Philly. "Mark's watching him."

"I know, I know." She sighs, and I can picture her pacing her studio. "He's an adult. He can manage his own health. We have to trust him."

"But?"

"But he's our baby." Her voice cracks slightly. "And he's so caught up in finally having his own show, his own spotlight..."

"That he's not taking care of himself." I finish what she can't. "I see it too."

"The excitement, the adrenaline..." She pauses. "It masks the symptoms sometimes. You remember what his doctor said."

"About how he might not feel the crash coming until it's too late." My hand tightens on the phone. "I tried to talk to him about Charlotte."

"Let me guess – he 'handled it'?"

"His exact words." I manage a weak laugh. "He's definitely our kid."

"Stubborn?"

"Independent." But we both hear the worry under the word. "God, Raine, I don't know how to do this. How to let him grow up but still..."

"Keep him safe?" Her voice softens. "Welcome to parenting adult children. Maya says we're terrible at it."

"Maya doesn't have a medical condition that could —" I cut myself off, unable to finish the thought.

"Will." She says my name like a lifeline. Like she has for twenty-five years. "Mark will be there. The whole crew knows his condition. He has all his backup supplies."

"I know." But the knot in my stomach won't ease. "I just wish..."

"That you could protect him forever?" Now she does laugh, soft and sad. "That's the thing about kids. At some point you have to trust them to protect themselves."

Chase's voice carries from the front of the bus – something about a radio interview in twenty minutes.

"I should go." But I don't want to. Don't want to lose this connection, this shared understanding of what it means to watch our son push himself too hard. "You'll try calling him?"

"Already planning to." I can hear her smile. "Right after his soundcheck, when he's coming down from the high of playing. He's always more reasonable then."

"Like someone else I know."

"Says the man who used to crash after shows and forget to eat entirely."

"That's different—"

"Because you're not diabetic?" Her tone sharpens slightly. "Will. He learned his performance habits from us. Both of us."

The truth of that hits hard. The way we both used to push ourselves, ride the adrenaline until we crashed. The example we set without meaning to.

"I'll check in later." I glance at the time – two hours until Pittsburgh. Two hours of trying not to count the miles between me and my son. "Love you."

"Love you too." She pauses. "Will? He'll be okay. He has to be."

But we both hear what she's not saying.

He has to be, because anything else is unthinkable.

The Pittsburgh arena is quiet and dark when we arrive, just the crew setting up for tomorrow's show. Modern Drummer's photographer is already waiting, getting establishing shots of the empty venue for their "Day in the Life" piece on me.

"Earth to Will." Chase waves a hand in front of my face. "They want some shots of you at the kit before the interview."

"Sorry." I try to focus on the present. On being professional. But my mind keeps drifting west, calculating the distance to Cleveland, the time until Lucas takes the stage.

"And, stop worrying so much. It's deepening your wrinkles, old man."

"That obvious?"

"Only to anyone with eyes." He hands me a coffee. "Mark texted from Cleveland. Said Lucas's readings were okay at lunch. A little low, but he ate something proper."

"You're checking up on him too?"

Chase's smile is gentle. "Kid's practically my

nephew. Besides, someone has to keep you functional for this press day."

My phone buzzes – a text from Lucas.

> LUCAS: Soundcheck crushed.
> Place is gonna be packed.

Then another.

> LUCAS: Also, numbers normal.
> Everyone can stop hovering.

"See?" Chase gestures at my phone. "He's good. Now can we talk about what angle you want to take for this interview? The whole 'legendary drummer watching his son follow in his footsteps' thing is gold."

I try to focus on the interview prep, on the story they want to tell. But another text comes through, this time from Mark.

> MARK: Made him eat before
> soundcheck. Still looking a little
> pale.

"Will." Chase's voice sharpens. "You're doing it again."

"Doing what?"

"That thing where you try to parent from two hundred miles away." He takes my phone gently. "He's got this. Mark's got this. You need to be here, now. This feature's important for both bands."

"I know." I run a hand through my hair, frustration building. "I just... something feels wrong."

"Because you're not there to protect him?" Chase's voice softens. "That's called being a father. It doesn't go away just because they grow up."

The photographer calls us over for setup shots at my kit. Chase stands, offering his hand.

"One thing at a time, drummer boy." He pulls me up. "That's all any of us can do."

I follow him to the kit, trying to push away the worry. Trying to focus on the interview, the photos, the story we're meant to be telling. But my phone feels heavy in my pocket, full of unspoken fears.

Another text buzzes just before we start.

RAINE: He's not answering my calls.

ME: Mark says he's sleeping before the show. Try to breathe. Try to trust.

I take a deep breath, picking up my sticks for the camera. The quiet of the empty arena should be familiar, professional. Just another day of press, of building both bands' profiles.

But all I can think about is another show, another city, and my son pushing himself too hard in his first real spotlight.

Chase catches my eye as I pose for another shot. Mouths, "He's got this."

I nod, twirling my sticks. Trying to believe it.

Some days, being a father means smiling for cameras in one city while leaving your heart in another.

I just pray we're all right about Lucas being ready for this.

Pray that this gnawing worry in my gut is just paranoia, not instinct.

Pray that tonight isn't the night we learn the difference.

## Nightmare

### WILL

HOURS LATER, the photographer is showing us the setup shots on his laptop, while the interviewer hurls questions at us when my phone rings. Mark never calls during shows – only texts – so my heart stops before I even see his name.

"What happened?" The words come out sharp, cutting through Chase's interview answer.

"He collapsed during the encore." Mark's voice is tight, controlled. Too controlled. "Cleveland Clinic. They've got him stabilized, but—"

"How bad?" I'm already moving, barely registering Chase following me.

"Sugar crashed hard. He skipped dinner, then with the heat and the adrenaline..." A pause. "Will, he seized before we could—"

"I'm coming." My hands are shaking as I gather

my jacket, my keys to a car that's not even here. "Two hours, maybe less—"

"I'll drive." Chase pats my shoulder smoothly, directing me to somebody's rental car, I don't even know whose it is. I can barely remember what city I'm in. "You're in no shape."

"They've got him on glucose drips," Mark continues. "Doctor says his levels were dangerously low. If we hadn't caught it when—"

"Don't." I can't hear that. Can't think about how close— "Just... stay with him. Please."

"Of course." A muffled conversation in the background. "They're taking him for more tests. I'll text you his room number."

The photographer is asking something about rescheduling, but Chase waves him off. Guides me toward the parking garage with a hand on my shoulder.

"Raine?" I manage as we reach my car.

"Already called her." Chase takes the driver's seat. "She's booking the first flight out."

My phone buzzes – Maya. Then again – Devon asking if they should come. Then Eliza, saying she'll handle tomorrow's press.

But all I can see is Lucas at four, banging on pots with wooden spoons. Lucas at twelve, terrified of his first insulin shot. Lucas last week in Charlotte, brushing off my concerns with that stubborn independence he gets from both his parents.

"He'll be okay." Chase pulls onto the highway, already pushing the speed limit. "Kids bounce back—"

"He seized, Chase." My voice breaks. "He's never... not since he was first diagnosed..."

"But they caught it." His tone is firm. "He's getting treatment. Mark was there."

Another text from Mark.

> MARK: Room 427, ICU. They're monitoring his glucose levels, running tests for organ function. He's stable.

"ICU." The word tastes like fear.

"Standard procedure." But Chase is pressing the accelerator harder. "They're just being thorough."

My phone rings again – Raine.

"Got a flight," she says without preamble. "Red eye. Lands early in the morning. The doctor says—"

"You talked to his doctor?"

"Of course I talked to his doctor." Her voice catches. "I'm his mother. I needed... I had to know..."

"How bad?" I need her precision. Her producer's eye for detail.

"Blood sugar was 32." Clinical words, but I hear the tremor. "He was conscious when they brought him in, but confused. The seizure lasted about a minute."

"Jesus." My hand tightens on the phone. "Did they say—"

"No permanent damage, they don't think." She takes a shaky breath. "But Will... he could have died. If Mark hadn't been watching..."

"I know." And I do. That's the thought I've been avoiding. The one I can't look at directly. "I'm on my way. Chase is driving."

"Good." Another tremor. "I can't... I need you to be there until I can..."

"I know that too." Twenty-five years of understanding catches in my throat. "I've got him. I promise."

"Nine hours, give or take," she whispers. "Just hold him for me for nine hours."

The line clicks off, and I stare at the highway stretching endlessly ahead. At the miles between me and my son.

Chase presses the accelerator harder.

Some distances can never be crossed fast enough.

The minutes crawl by like hours. Every red light is an eternity. Every slow car in our way feels like a personal attack. Chase weaves through traffic with focused intensity, but it's not fast enough. Nothing could be fast enough.

My phone keeps lighting up with updates from Mark.

MARK: Still running tests He's more alert now Asking for you. Worried about missing tomorrow's show.

That last one hits like a punch to the gut. Of course he's worried about the show. Of course that's what he's thinking about, even in the fucking ICU. He's our son, after all.

"Remember his first real show?" Chase's voice breaks through my spiral. "The showcase at the Whiskey years ago with that shitty band he was in?"

"Chase—"

"He was so nervous backstage." He takes a curve faster than strictly legal. "Until you told him about your first time at the Whiskey. About how you threw up before going on."

"Twice." The memory comes unbidden. "In the alley behind the kitchen."

"And he laughed." Chase glances at me. "Said at least his nerves couldn't be worse than his old man's."

"He was eighteen." My throat tightens. "Did his blood sugar check right there at the kit. So proud to handle it himself."

"He's still handling it." Chase's voice is gentle. "This is just a setback."

Another text from Mark.

MARK: Doctor says glucose levels stabilizing. Still monitoring kidney function.

"Kidney function." The words come out sharp with fear.

"Standard for severe hypoglycemia." Chase

sounds so certain I almost believe him. "They're just being thorough."

My phone rings – Maya again. I almost let it go to voicemail, but Chase gives me a look.

"Dad?" Her voice is small, young. "Devon's got a bag packed. We can be there by morning if—"

"Stay in LA." The words hurt to say. "Your mother will be here in a few hours. No point in everyone—"

"He's my brother." Steel enters her tone. "And he's in the ICU."

"Maya." I close my eyes, seeing her at fourteen, holding her baby brother's hand in the hospital. Teaching him to check his sugar. Watching him from side stage at every show. "Please. Let us handle this part. If anything changes..."

"Promise?" She sounds young again. Scared.

"Promise." I swallow hard. "I'll text as soon as I see him."

After we hang up, Chase merges onto I-80, pushing the speedometer higher, taking another curve fast. "Remember when you played through that fever in Toronto?"

"That was different—"

"Because you're not diabetic?" His tone sharpens slightly. "Will. He learned his performance ethic from you. From both of you."

The truth of that silences me. All those years of

pushing through exhaustion, of putting the show first. All the examples we set without meaning to.

Another text from Mark.

> MARK: He's asking about his kit. About tomorrow's show. Told him not a chance.

Then-

> MARK: He's scared, man. Really scared. Trying not to show it, but...

"Faster," I whisper, and Chase pushes the car harder.

Sometimes, being a father means facing every mistake you never knew you were making.

The Cleveland Clinic's ICU is too bright, too sterile, too much like that first time when Lucas was twelve and we were learning words like "ketoacidosis" and "glucose monitoring." My hands shake as I write my name on the visitor log, as I pin on the parent badge that feels simultaneously wrong and terrifyingly right.

Mark meets us at the elevator, looking older than I've ever seen him.

"He's more stable." The words come fast, like he's been rehearsing them. "Doctor says the seizure didn't cause any damage. They're still monitoring his kidneys, but his numbers are coming up..."

"Mark." I grab his shoulder, steadying us both. "Thank you. For being there. For catching it..."

"Should have caught it sooner." His voice roughens. "Saw him skipping dinner, but he said he'd grabbed something after soundcheck. Then during the encore, he started missing hits. Just slightly, but..."

"You got him here." Chase's hand lands on my back, supporting. "That's what matters."

Room 427 looms ahead, and suddenly I can't breathe. Can't move. Can't face what's waiting behind that door.

"Will." Mark's voice gentles. "He needs his dad."

The room is dim except for the glow of monitors. Lucas looks impossibly young in the hospital bed, all that rockstar confidence stripped away. IVs trail from both arms, and the steady beep of machines measures my son's heartbeat with mechanical precision.

"Dad?" His voice is raspy, small. "I'm sorry. I really fucked up."

"Hey." I'm moving before I realize it, gathering him as carefully as I can around the tubes and wires. "None of that. Just... God, Lucas."

"The show tomorrow..." He starts, but I cut him off.

"Is canceled." I pull back enough to see his face, to really look at him. At the shadows under his eyes, the pallor of his skin. At all the signs I should have seen coming. The signs I *did* see coming, but could do nothing about. "No arguments."

"But—"

"Lucas." I rarely use that tone with him anymore, but it comes naturally now. "You seized. Your blood sugar was 32. You could have—" My voice cracks, and I have to stop. Have to breathe.

"I know." He looks down, fingers picking at his blanket. "I just... everything was going so well. The crowd was insane, and I didn't want to miss a moment of it..."

"By missing all the moments after it?" The words come sharper than I mean them to. Or, maybe I do mean it. "By risking everything for one show?"

"Like you've never done that?" But there's no heat in his voice. Just exhaustion. Fear.

"And that's on me." I sink into the chair beside his bed, keeping his hand in mine. "All those times I pushed too hard, played through anything... God, Lucas, what kind of example did we set?"

"A professional one." His attempt at a smile fails. "The show must go on, right?"

"Not like this." I squeeze his hand, careful of the IV. "Never like this."

His monitors beep, and a nurse comes in to check

readings. To adjust something in his drip. To remind him gently that he needs rest.

"Mom's coming?" He asks after she leaves, and suddenly he's my little boy again. Scared and trying not to show it.

"Lands at six." I brush his hair back, the way I used to when he was small. "Chase is picking her up."

"She's going to be so mad."

"Terrified," I correct softly. "We both are. Were. Are..."

"I really thought I could handle it." His voice catches. "That I knew my limits..."

"I know." And I do. God, I do. "But sometimes being professional means knowing when to stop. When to say no."

"Even if it lets people down?"

"You being alive doesn't let anyone down." My voice roughens. "You being safe, and *alive,* matters more than any show, any crowd, any moment on stage."

He's quiet for a long moment, and I think he's drifting off. But then, so softly I almost miss it:

"I was scared, Dad. When it started happening. When I couldn't... when my hands wouldn't..."

"I know, buddy." I kiss his forehead, breathing in the scent of him. Living, breathing, here. "I know."

The monitors beep steadily. Outside, I can hear Mark and Chase talking quietly with the doctor. Can hear the normal sounds of a hospital at night.

But all I can focus on is my son's pulse under my fingers. The rise and fall of his chest. The miracle of him, still here, still fighting.

The guilt of the example I've set rolls through me in waves, threatening to drown me.

*Keep fucking fighting.*

# *Partly Cloudy*

## RAINE

**THE FLIGHT FEELS ENDLESS.** Every minute stretches like hours as I stare at the last photo Lucas sent me – grinning from his kit during soundcheck, so alive with excitement I couldn't see how close to the edge he was.

Or, didn't want to see.

Hours in the air has given me time to think about and reconsider everything. About how somethings change, and how some don't. Old patterns reappear, or just make themselves known again. And the pain that comes with them stabs me in the heart.

*Deep.*

I should have known this would happen. I think I *did* know that this would happen, somehow. That all of my worst fears would come true. I just didn't want to believe it. I wanted to believe that things were different now. And because of it, I nearly lost my son.

*My baby.*

Chase meets me at baggage claim, and one look at his face tells me everything I need to know. My fears as a mother are cynically validated.

"He's stable," he says before I can ask. "Glucose levels are normalizing. Will's with him."

*Will.*

The name sits like acid in my throat. Who was supposed to keep this from happening. Who promised to watch him, to make sure... just like he used to promise to be there for recitals, for school events, for all the moments that always came second to the band.

"What happened?" My voice comes out sharp, brittle. I'm trying to cover my fear, but failing miserably. "Really happened?"

Chase guides me toward the parking garage, his hand gentle on my arm. "He skipped dinner. Was too excited about the show, about finally headlining..."

"And no one noticed?" The words taste like old fears, like memories of another hospital room, another time Will chose wrong. "No one thought to check why he was skipping meals before a show?"

"Mark tried." Chase's voice is careful now. Like he can hear the past creeping into my tone. "Made him eat lunch, kept protein bars by the kit..."

"But Will wasn't there." The accusation burns. "He was doing that magazine piece instead. Just like always – the band first, press first, everything else second. Mark isn't his fucking father."

"Raine." His tone holds warning. "Don't. Not now. This isn't like before—"

"Isn't it?" My laugh holds no humor. "Our son is in the ICU, Chase. He seized. He could have—" My voice breaks. "And where was his father? In Pittsburgh. Doing press. Like nothing's changed at all."

"That's not fair." He opens the car door for me, ever the gentleman even in crisis. "Will's destroyed over this. He couldn't even drive himself here—"

"Good." The coldness in my voice surprises even me. "Maybe he'll finally understand what it feels like. To get that call. To be too far away to help."

The drive to the hospital blurs. Cleveland's streets are empty at this hour, and Chase takes advantage, pushing the speed limit. My phone keeps lighting up with updates from Maya, from Devon, from what feels like the entire industry asking if we need anything.

But all I can see is Lucas at twelve, so scared of that first insulin shot. Lucas practicing his readings until they were automatic. Lucas promising he could handle tour life, handle his health, handle everything... just like I used to promise myself I could handle Will's absences. His priorities. His choices.

"He's in 427." Chase parks in the emergency lot. "Will's been there since we arrived. Hasn't left his side."

"*Now* he's there." The words come out like shards of glass. "When it's already too late. When—"

"Stop." Chase's voice sharpens. "This isn't twenty years ago, Raine. This isn't about missed recitals or—"

"No." I grab my purse, needing to move. To do something with this familiar anger. "It's worse. Because he promised it would be different this time. That family came first this time. That he'd changed."

The ICU is too bright, too much like every fear I've had since Lucas was diagnosed. Will stands when I enter the room, and for a moment I see the hope in his eyes. The relief at seeing me. The need for connection in crisis.

It makes me furious. Makes me want to scream about how he doesn't get to need me now. Doesn't get to play concerned father, now that the worst has already happened.

But then I see Lucas, pale against the hospital sheets, IVs in both arms, and everything else disappears except my baby boy.

"Baby." I'm at his side in an instant, touching his face, his hands, needing to feel him warm and alive. "I'm here. Mom's here."

"I'm okay." His voice is weak, but he tries to smile. "Really. Just being dramatic."

"Your blood sugar was 32." My voice catches. "You seized. That's not dramatic, that's—"

"I know." He looks down, and suddenly he's my little boy again. The one who used to crawl into my lap after bad dreams. After his father missed another dinner. Another promise. "I messed up."

"We all did." Will's voice is rough. He moves to touch my shoulder but seems to think better of it. *Good.* "The doctor says—"

"When did you last check his readings?" The question comes out like a weapon. "Before you left for Pittsburgh? Before the press became more important than—"

"Raine." His tone holds hurt. Like he has any right to feel wounded when our son is the one in a hospital bed. "Don't. Please."

"Don't what?" I stroke Lucas's hair, unable to look at Will. Unable to face the familiar way he's trying to make this okay. To smooth things over like he always did. "Don't ask why no one was monitoring him? Why you were in another city when he needed you? Why nothing ever really changes?"

"Mom." Lucas tries to sit up, but the monitors protest. "It's not Dad's fault. He wasn't even—"

"Exactly." The word hangs between us, heavy with two decades of disappointment. "He wasn't there. Again."

"I was doing press." Will's voice tightens. "For both bands. You know that. We discussed—"

"We discussed you watching him." My hands shake as I adjust Lucas's blanket, needing to do something, to fix something. "Making sure he didn't push too hard. That he didn't get caught up in—"

"In being exactly like us?" Will moves closer, and I can feel him trying to make me understand. Just like he used to try to explain missed birthdays, canceled plans, all the times the band came first. "In putting the show first, like we taught him to?"

"Don't." Now I do look at him, letting him see how this feels like every other time he's tried to rationalize his choices. "Don't make this about us. About patterns. About history. This is about our son being in the ICU because everyone was too busy chasing success to see what was happening."

"Guys." Lucas's voice is small between us. "Please. I'm the one who messed up. Who didn't check. Who thought I could handle—"

"Of course you thought that." I kiss his forehead, needing to touch him. To know he's really okay even as my heart breaks at how familiar this all feels. "Because that's what we showed you. What *he* taught you. That the show always comes first. That success matters more than—"

"Raine." Chase's voice from the doorway makes us all jump. "Coffee run. Help me carry?"

It's a transparent excuse, but I take it. Need it. Need space from the machines measuring my son's heartbeat. From the man I thought had changed looking at me with those same apologetic eyes I remember from a thousand disappointments.

"Go." Lucas squeezes my hand. "I'm not going anywhere. Doctor's orders."

"Five minutes." I kiss him again, memorizing his warmth. His aliveness. Trying not to think about how close we came to losing him while his father was doing press in another city.

Will starts to speak as I pass, but I can't. Can't hear his explanations or his guilt or his love. Not when they feel like echoes of every other time he's tried to make things right after putting everything else first.

Chase waits until we're in the elevator to speak.

"That was unfair."

"Our son—"

"Is an adult who made his own choices." His voice gentles. "Will's destroying himself over this already. He doesn't need you—"

"Need me what?" The elevator feels too small suddenly. Too confined. Like all the ways I've felt trapped by his promises before. "Need me to pretend this isn't exactly what always happens? That he doesn't always choose wrong when it matters most?"

"That's not what this is, and you know it." Chase hits the lobby button harder than necessary. "He's been there for Lucas through everything. Through diagnosis, through learning to manage—"

"Until he wasn't." The words taste like old tears. "Until something more important came along. Just like always."

"A magazine piece about both bands isn't—"

"It's never just one thing, Chase." My voice catches. "It's press, then tour, then the next album. It's always something. And we're always supposed to understand. To wait. To accept that next time will be different."

"This isn't fair, and you know it." He guides me toward the coffee shop. "Will's not that person anymore. You know he's not."

"Do I?" The question comes out small. Scared. "Because from where I'm standing, it looks exactly the same. Choose wrong, apologize, promise to do better, repeat."

"You're letting fear make you cruel." Chase's voice softens. "And you're going to regret it when you're thinking clearly again."

"Maybe." I wrap my arms around myself, suddenly cold. "Or maybe I'm finally seeing clearly for the first time since we started this again. Maybe some patterns don't change, no matter how much we want them to."

The walk back to the ICU feels longer. Heavier. Each step a choice between fear and love, between blame and understanding.

Between trusting again and protecting my heart from what feels inevitable.

Lucas is sleeping when we return, his face finally peaceful. Will stands at the window, and something in his posture – the defeat in his shoulders, the way his hands clench – reminds me so much of other hospital rooms, other apologies, other promises that never quite held.

"Here." I set his coffee on the windowsill, careful not to touch him. Careful not to let myself feel anything except the fear and anger keeping me upright.

"Thanks." His voice is rough, tired. Like he's aged years in hours. Like he always sounded after missing something important, after trying to make it right.

We stand in silence, watching our son breathe. Watching the monitors confirm what we need most – that he's alive, stable, still here. Despite everything. Despite choices. Despite patterns that never seem to break.

"I'm sorry." His voice comes soft, familiar. Too familiar.

"Don't." I keep my eyes on Lucas, on the rise and fall of his chest. "Just... don't. I can't hear that right now. Can't do this dance again."

"Raine—"

"I need to call Maya." I move toward the door, needing space. Air. Room to breathe around this feeling of history repeating. "Update her on his numbers."

"Let me—"

"No." The word comes sharp. Final. "I've got it. I've always got it. That's how this works, remember?"

I don't wait for his response. Can't bear to see the hurt in his eyes or the way he'll try to make this better.

To make me understand.

To promise things will be different.

# Lioness

## WILL

**THE COFFEE GROWS** cold on the windowsill where Raine left it. Like everything else she's left untouched since arriving – my attempts to explain, to connect, to bridge this gulf that feels like twenty years of accumulated hurt crashing back at once.

I can't blame her. Not really. The look in her eyes when she walked into the ICU room – I've seen it before. Too many times. After missed recitals, forgotten anniversaries, all the moments I put the band first because I thought I had to. Because that's what success demanded.

But this isn't the same. I'm not the same.

Lucas stirs in his sleep, and I'm at his side instantly, checking his monitor. The numbers are steady now, but I can't stop seeing them from last night. Can't stop hearing Mark's voice on the phone, tight with panic. Can't stop feeling the way my world tilted on its axis when I realized I was in the wrong city at the wrong time.

Again.

"Dad?" Lucas's voice is scratchy, weak. "Where's Mom?"

"Calling Maya." I adjust his blanket, needing to do something with my hands. Needing to be useful in some way that matters. "How're you feeling?"

"Like I really fucked up." His smile is wan. "Like I let everyone down."

"No." The word comes fierce. "You didn't let anyone down. I'm the one who—"

"Don't." He sounds so much like his mother it makes my chest ache. "This isn't your fault. You can't be everywhere at once."

But I should have been here. Should have seen this coming. Should have done something, anything, to prevent this.

The irony doesn't escape me. All those years I spent choosing wrong, putting the band first, thinking there would always be time to make it up later. Now, when I'm finally getting it right – being there for Lucas's shows, rearranging tours around family, actually putting them first – one magazine piece brings it all crashing down.

Makes Raine look at me like she used to. Like she can't trust me with her heart. With our kids' hearts.

"She's scared." Lucas's voice breaks through my

spiral. "Mom, I mean. This isn't about you, not really. It's about almost losing—"

He cuts himself off, but I hear the rest. About almost losing him. About how close we came to every parent's worst nightmare.

"I know." I sink into the chair beside his bed. "But she's not wrong, Lucas. I should have been there. Should have seen the signs. Should have—"

"What? Been in two places at once?" He shifts, wincing. "The magazine piece was for my band too, Dad. You were trying to help both of us succeed."

"At what cost?" The question comes raw, honest. "What good is success if—"

If I lose them again. If I make Raine look at me like that again. If I become the man I used to be, the one who always choses wrong when it matters most.

The door opens, and Raine slips back in. She doesn't meet my eyes, but I see the tension in her shoulders. The way she holds herself like she's bracing for another disappointment. Another excuse. Another promise I can't keep.

"Maya's apparently on her way." Her voice is controlled. Professional. Like she's talking to a session musician, not the man she was falling in love with again just yesterday. "Devon insisted."

"They don't have to—"

"She needs to see her brother." The unspoken accusation hangs between us.

*Unlike some people, Maya shows up when family needs her.*

"Mom." Lucas's tone holds warning. "Stop."

"I'm just saying—"

"I know what you're saying." His voice strengthens. "And it's not fair. Dad's not who he was back then. You know he's not."

"Do I?" But something flickers in her eyes. Doubt maybe. Or fear of being wrong about being right. "Because from where I'm standing—"

"You're standing in the wrong place then." The words come out before I can stop them. "Looking at the wrong version of me. The wrong pattern."

She does look at me then, really look at me, and for a moment I see past the anger to the terror underneath. The mother who almost lost her son. The woman who's afraid of trusting me again only to be disappointed.

"Am I?" Her voice catches. "Because it feels exactly the same, Will. The excuses, the choices, the—"

"The man?" I stand, needing her to see me. Really see me. "Because I'm not him anymore, Raine. Haven't been for a long time."

"Guys." Lucas tries to sit up, but the movement pulls his IV. "Please don't do this here."

He's right. This isn't the place. Not with our son in a hospital bed. Not with monitors beeping out the rhythm of how close we came to losing everything that matters.

"I'm going to get more ice." I move toward the door, giving Raine space. Giving myself space to breathe around the familiar ache of disappointing her. "Need anything?"

She shakes her head, already focused on Lucas. Already building those walls I used to know so well. The ones that kept her safe when I couldn't be trusted with her heart.

In the hallway, I lean against the wall, letting myself feel everything I've been trying to contain. The fear of almost losing Lucas. The pain of Raine's anger. The bitter taste of being blamed for something I've spent years changing.

Chase finds me there, ever the best friend who sees too much.

"She'll remember." He hands me a fresh coffee. "When the fear dies down. When she can see clearly again. She'll remember who you are now."

"Will she?" I take the coffee but don't drink it. "Or will she just keep seeing who I was? Keep waiting for me to prove her right?"

"You're different now."

"Am I?" The question comes quiet. Raw. "Because I still wasn't there when it mattered. Still chose wrong when it counted."

"You *choose* to help both your kids succeed." Chase's voice holds certainty I wish I felt. "To be there for Maya's career and Lucas's band. You're trying to be everything for everyone, and sometimes that means being in the wrong place at the wrong time."

"Try telling Raine that."

"She knows." He squeezes my shoulder. "Deep down, past the fear, she knows. That's what scares her most."

I think about the way she looked at me in the studio not that long ago. The way she was starting to trust again. To believe in us again.

Now this.

"I can't lose them again." The words come rough, honest. "Can't be that man again."

"You're not." Chase's certainty steadies me. "And when she's ready to see past her fear, she'll remember that too."

I hope to whatever god there is that he's right. Hope she'll remember the man I've become, not just the one who let her down so many times before.

Hope love really is stronger than fear, than memory, than the patterns we're both afraid of repeating.

Even if right now, watching her rebuild those walls, it feels like history winning after all.

# Numb

RAINE

I NEED space from this hospital room. From the beeping monitors. From Will's careful distance and Lucas's worried glances between us.

"I'm getting coffee." I stand, needing to move. To breathe. "Real coffee, not hospital sludge."

"Mom—" Lucas starts, but Maya cuts him off, having just arrived from parking the car.

"Let me settle in first," she says, already claiming the chair I was just in next to his bed. "Then we can all take turns getting actual food. Devon's right behind me, just taking a work call."

Will doesn't look up from his phone – probably checking Lucas's readings for the hundredth time. We've barely spoken all day, both of us too careful, too aware of the fragile peace we're maintaining for Lucas's sake.

The hospital corridor feels too sterile. I'm halfway to the elevator when I hear footsteps behind me.

"Mind if I join?" Devon, briefcase in hand, phone call apparently finished. "Need caffeine after that long flight."

He looks every inch the corporate lawyer – suit slightly rumpled from the flight, tie loosened, but that same analytical focus Maya says makes him lethal in negotiations.

"The cafeteria's terrible," I warn, but he falls into step beside me.

"Can't be worse than the coffee at the courthouse." He checks his phone briefly. "Though speaking as someone who's spent too much time in hospitals lately with case prep, the coffee cart in the lobby is usually better."

We ride down in companionable silence. Devon's not one for small talk – it's one of the things I've always appreciated about him. He observes, analyzes, speaks when he has something worth saying.

"You know," he says as we wait in line at the cart, "I've been going over old contracts all week. Partnership dissolutions mostly."

I raise an eyebrow at the apparent non sequitur.

"It's interesting," he continues, ordering his coffee with practiced efficiency. "How often people let old patterns dictate new situations. Even when circumstances have completely changed."

"Devon—"

"Just an observation." His tone stays professional, measured. "From someone who's watched Will completely restructure a major tour to accommodate Lucas's health. Who's seen him prioritize family over career consistently since I've known him."

"You don't know—"

"What he was like before? No, I don't." He pays for both our coffees, waving off my protest. "But I know who he is now. And from a purely objective standpoint, his actions demonstrate a clear pattern of changed behavior."

I almost smile despite myself. "Are you lawyering me?"

"Presenting relevant evidence." But there's a glint of humor in his eyes. "Would you like me to submit it in writing?"

We find a quiet corner of the lobby, away from the bustle of visitors and staff.

"I'm scared," I admit quietly. "Of trusting again. Of believing things are different."

"Understandable." He sips his coffee with the air of someone used to having difficult conversations. "But maybe the question isn't whether he's changed, but whether you're willing to see it."

The truth of that hits hard.

"When did you get so insightful about relationships?"

"I analyze patterns for a living." He shrugs. "And your family's patterns have shifted significantly since

I've known you. Except perhaps this one – where fear of the past overshadows evidence of the present."

My phone buzzes – Lucas's latest readings, steady and strong. Above it, I see Will's text from earlier in the day. I guess texting was safer than speaking out loud. I can't blame him for that.

> WILL: Numbers looking good. Let me know if you want me to take next watch so you can rest.*

Still taking care of everyone. Still trying to do the right thing. Still being the man he's become, not the one he was. Is that right? Have I been wrong about all this?

"Think about it," Devon says, standing. "And not just as a mother who's terrified for her son. But as someone who might be letting old fears cost her something important."

He heads back upstairs, leaving me with cooling coffee and uncomfortable truths.

Maybe it's time to stop looking for old patterns and start seeing new ones.

Even if that means being brave enough to trust again.

I stare at my coffee, Devon's words sinking in. He's right – I'm looking for old patterns because they're familiar. Because fear is easier than trust. Because blaming Will is simpler than admitting how terrified I am of almost losing Lucas.

The adrenaline of the crisis is finally fading, leaving me hollow and clear-headed for the first time since that call. The facts are simple: Lucas is stable. He made a mistake, like any young performer might. Like I used to, pushing myself too hard in studios, forgetting to eat during marathon sessions.

And Will...

I close my eyes, really thinking about the past few months. The way he rearranged the entire tour schedule around Lucas's health needs. How he checks readings obsessively, keeps protein bars stashed everywhere, learned every detail of diabetes management. The way he's put family first in ways that would have seemed impossible twenty years ago.

This isn't the same man who missed Maya's debate finals for a show. Who scheduled tours without considering holidays or birthdays. Who always chose the band first because he thought that's what being successful meant.

This is a father who drives three blocks out of his way every night just to check my condo. Who helps Maya with wedding details even though it must hurt, knowing I'll sing our song. Who's been giving Lucas exactly what he needs – trust to manage his own health, while still maintaining that safety net.

And what have I given him in return? Blame. Anger. The assumption that he'll always be who he was, never who he's become.

My phone buzzes – another text from Will.

> WILL: Got Lucas to eat something proper. Numbers steady. Take your time, get some air. We've got him.

*We've got him.*

Not just him watching our son. Not just him taking care of everything. But us, together, like we've learned to be. Like we were becoming again before fear made me push him away.

Through the lobby windows, I watch families coming and going. Some celebrating new life, some grieving losses, some just getting through another day of waiting and hoping. All of them dealing with their own patterns, their own fears.

But fear doesn't have to win. Doesn't have to dictate choices. Doesn't have to blind me to the truth right in front of me.

Lucas is an adult. A successful musician managing his own career, his own health, his own life. My job isn't to protect him from everything anymore – it's to trust him to protect himself, while being there when he needs support.

Just like Will's been doing all along.

I pull out my phone, stare at his last message. At all the messages through this crisis – steady updates, careful distance, still taking care of everyone even while I've been punishing him for old sins he's long since atoned for.

My fingers hover over the keys. It would be so

easy to keep this wall up. To stay safe in my anger and fear. To keep seeing the patterns I expect instead of the truth in front of me.

But some patterns need to break. Even if just a little bit for now.

> ME: Thank you. For taking care of him. For taking care of everyone.

His response comes quickly.

> WILL: Always. Even when you're angry. Even when you're scared. Even when you don't trust me to be different.

The truth of that hits hard. How he's stayed steady even while I've been pushing him away. How he's kept proving himself even while I've been determined not to see it.

> ME: I do trust you. I think. I'm just terrible at showing it when I'm terrified.

A longer pause.

> WILL: I know. I remember. But I'm not going anywhere this time. No matter how hard you push.

And that's the real difference, isn't it? Not just who he's become, but who we've become. Better versions of ourselves, even if we sometimes forget in moments of crisis.

Even if I sometimes forget.

I stand, suddenly needing to see him. To really see him, not just the mistakes he used to make or the fears I can't seem to shake.

I need to try to be as brave about love as he's been about change.

Can I even do that now? I'm not so sure.

Honestly, I don't feel brave at all. I still feel weak. I still feel old hurts like they're fresh. I'm still afraid, no, *terrified* to trust again. Despite what's changed. Despite what's right in front of me and can see with my own eyes. Despite what I know deep down in my very soul.

Despite everything, I don't see a way past it.

Not yet. Not quite.

Fear of everything going horribly wrong is pulsing through my veins no matter how hard I try to stop it. Every nerve in my body is still on high alert, ready for the next shoe to drop. The next disappointment.

The next hurt.

## Dynamite

### WILL

**LUCAS'S NUMBERS ARE STEADY.** Have been for hours. But I can't stop checking the app, can't stop watching for any sign of change. Can't stop trying to control something in this situation that feels completely out of my control.

"Dad." Maya's voice is gentle. "Go find Mom."

"She needs space." The words come automatically. The same way I've been giving her space all day, trying not to push, trying not to make things worse.

"No," Devon says from his spot by the window. "She needs you to show her nothing's changed. That you're still steady, even when she's not."

I look at Lucas, but he just nods. "Go. I've got enough babysitters for now."

The hospital corridors feel endless as I search for her. I know she got coffee – the basic tasks we all do during crisis, pretending normalcy. Pretending we're not falling apart.

I find her in the lobby, staring at her phone like it holds answers. She looks exhausted, small, nothing like the fierce woman who stormed in this morning ready to protect our son from everything. Including me.

"Hey." My voice comes soft, careful still.

She looks up, and something in her expression makes my heart stop. The anger's gone, replaced by something that looks a lot like understanding. Like remembering.

"I've been unfair." Her voice catches.

"You've been scared." I move closer, drawn by the tears in her eyes. "We both have been."

"But I've been punishing you for who you were, not seeing who you are." She stands, takes a step toward me. "The man who rearranges tours for family. Who checks streets every night. Who loves our kids enough to let them make their own choices, even when it terrifies you."

"Raine—"

"Let me finish?" She's close enough now that I can smell her perfume, see the silver in her hair catching the fluorescent lights. "I got so caught up in old patterns, in old fears... I couldn't see how different everything is now. How different you are."

"We both are." I reach for her hand, relief flooding through me when she lets me take it.

"Better at this. Better at understanding what matters."

"I'm sorry." The words come with tears now. "For blaming you. For not trusting you. I just got caught up—"

I pull her into my arms, unable to bear the distance anymore. She comes reluctantly, pressing her face to my chest like she used to when the world got too big, too scary.

"I know why you were scared." I breathe in the scent of her hair, letting myself feel everything I've been holding back. "God, Raine, I know. When I got that call..."

She pulls back enough to look at me, really look at me. "Even while I've been—"

"Being a terrified mother?" I brush tears from her cheeks. "Being scared of trusting me again? Being human?"

She laughs softly, the sound watery but real. Something dark passes her eyes. Memories of the past. Both far and near. "Being impossible."

"Good thing I love impossible." I kiss her forehead, feeling her melt slightly against me. Almost letting herself give in, but not quite. "Love you. Even when you're pushing me away. Even when you're scared. Even when you forget who we are now."

She stiffens at my words. Maybe I said too much when I said I loved her. Maybe it's too soon after everything. Too much.

"And who are we now?" The fear is back, and it's almost tangible; it's so heavy.

"Better." I tilt her chin up, needing her to see my truth. "Stronger. Ready to face anything, as long as we do it together."

"We should get back." She tries to step away, her gaze dropping, but I don't let her. Not yet. "Before Lucas sends out a search party."

"Let him." I hold her closer, needing another moment of just us. It's starting to feel like every bridge we just mended is made of paper mache, and it's falling apart. "He's got Maya and Devon. And his numbers are good."

"I know...I just..." She moves away, and this time I have to let her, my hands now cold with her absence. "I need—"

She doesn't finish, but heads toward the elevators, hugging herself with her head down. With every step she takes away from me, I can feel everything we just said to each other start to dissipate like fog in the sun. Not that what we said wasn't true, but it's just part of the emotional roller coaster we're both stuck on. Our feelings are all over the place.

Even though she says now that she doesn't blame me, I know that's only a half-truth. I can still feel the mistrust lingering between us. Even though she apologized for only seeing the old me, I know she's still not seeing me now. Not completely.

As I eventually follow Raine back to the room,

everything feels tenuous. Ephemeral. Temporary. I've gone from guilt and hurt, to what I thought was forgiveness, back to guilt and hurt in the matter of a few heartbeats.

I'm right back where I started, and I don't know if I have any fight left in me.

*I can't be the only one fighting for us.*

# Show Me the Way You Love

## WILL

"I STILL CAN'T BELIEVE they put your old leather pants in a museum." Lucas shakes his head as we approach the Rock Hall's glass pyramid. He's moving slower than usual, but the color's back in his face, and his readings have been stable for twenty-four hours. "Like, an actual museum. With a plaque and everything."

"They were quite something." Raine's voice holds that careful neutrality I've been hearing since the hospital. She walks slightly ahead with Lucas, keeping space between us I don't know how to bridge. "Even if they did split on stage in Seattle."

"That was Mark's fault." I try for lightness, for any connection. "He told me they'd stretch."

"Sure, blame the guitarist." Mark holds the door, hovering near Lucas without being obvious about it.

"I distinctly remember someone saying they made his ass look great."

"They did though." Chase winks at the ticket taker who's trying not to look starstruck. "Still would, if someone hadn't gained a few pounds since '99."

The young woman at tickets straightens when she sees us, recognition lighting her face. "Oh my god. I was at the show the other night. The one where..." She trails off, glancing at Lucas. "I mean, I've been following your recovery on social media. Everyone has. Are you okay?"

"Getting there." Lucas manages a smile, though I see the way he leans slightly on Maya. Still tired. Still healing. "Thanks for asking."

"I just..." She fumbles with her phone. "Would it be completely unprofessional to ask for a photo? My bandmates will never believe you guys are actually here. I'm a drummer, too."

"Only if we get you in it too," Chase grins, ever the charmer. "Since you're part of Cleveland's music scene."

She blushes. "I wouldn't say that. My band's just starting out. Though seeing Another Angel with Lucas on drums... before everything happened... it was inspiring."

Something passes between her and Lucas – that understanding of being young and hungry and thinking you're invincible. I catch Raine watching them, see her squeeze Lucas's shoulder. Maternal instinct warring with the need to let him find his own path.

"Welcome to the Rock and Roll Hall of Fame." The ticket girl – Amanda, her nametag reads – hands us our passes after the photos. "The Incendiary Ink exhibit is on the third floor. Recently expanded after the induction ceremony."

The elevator feels crowded with all of us – family in various configurations, bound by blood and choice and music. Maya chatters about wedding details while Devon examines every display we pass, that analytical lawyer's mind cataloging everything. But I'm watching Mark, the way his hands keep clenching and unclenching, the silence that feels heavier than usual.

The Incendiary Ink exhibit spans our whole career: demo tapes, handwritten lyrics, setlists from legendary shows. Twenty-five years of history under glass, including moments I'd almost forgotten.

"Oh my god." Lucas stops at a particular display, grinning. "Is that me?"

The photo shows him at maybe three, sitting at my kit with Maya helping him hold the sticks. Both of them so small, so innocent, surrounded by the controlled chaos of a recording studio. Raine's in the shot too, watching from the console, love clear on her face.

She turns away from that photo now.

My heart cracks.

"Your first session." I move closer to Lucas, careful not to crowd Raine's space. "We couldn't find a sitter, so..."

"So we brought you to work." Her voice holds an edge. "Like always. The job came first."

"Mom—"

"I'm just saying." She adjusts his jacket with careful hands.

Mark clears his throat. "Hey, remember this?" He points to another display – his original blue mohawk preserved somehow in a photo series.

But the attempt at distraction falls flat. The air feels thick with everything we're not saying. Everything we might never say now.

"Look at this." Devon's already moved to the next case, examining the guitars with professional interest, clearly trying to shift the mood. "Original '59 Les Paul Custom. The one from the first album cover?"

"Good eye." Mark's voice carries real animation for the first time today. "Bought it used for eight hundred bucks. Worth about eighty thousand now."

"If you ever sold it." Chase grins. "Which you won't."

"Some things are worth more than money." But Mark's brief energy fades, replaced by that distant look again. That bone-deep exhaustion I recognize too well.

Maya's already pulling out her phone. "Mom,

Dad, get in front of the gold record display. The lighting's perfect."

"Always the director." Lucas laughs, but I see him check his phone monitoring app first. Always aware now, even when trying to seem casual.

Raine notices too. We all do. But she just squeezes his arm, trusting him to handle it. Trusting somebody at least. Even if it's not me.

Not yet.

"Here." Devon takes Maya's phone, gesturing all of us to get into the frame. "Family photo time."

*Family.*

The word settles warm in my chest as Raine fits against me, as Lucas leans on his sister, as Chase drags a reluctant Mark into the shot. All of us reflected in the glass protecting our history, creating new memories over old ones.

The moment breaks when Lucas's monitor beeps – time for a snack. We all freeze, that ingrained panic response, but he just pulls a protein bar from his pocket. Handling it. Managing his own health while letting us hover just enough to feel useful.

"The cafe here is supposed to be good," Maya suggests. "We could all use a break."

Mark starts to step back, that familiar need to escape written in every line of his body. But Chase catches his arm. "When's the last time you ate actual food?"

"I'm fine."

"Sure you are." Chase's voice holds the same gentle firmness he used to use on me. "Totally fine. Just like Will was fine before his shoulder surgery. Like I was fine before rehab."

Mark stares at the cases, at our history preserved behind glass. At younger versions of ourselves who thought we could handle anything. Who didn't know our own limits until we crashed through them.

"Cafe," I say firmly, recognizing too much of myself in his expression. "All of us."

He starts to protest, but his hands are shaking again. Like Lucas's did before Cleveland. Like mine used to, pushing too hard for too long.

The museum cafe is surprisingly busy for a weekday afternoon. Maya snags us a corner table while Devon studies the menu with the same intensity he brings to contract negotiations.

"They have actual food," he announces, pleased. "Not just museum snacks."

"Good." Chase practically pushes Mark into a chair. "Because some of us are going to eat something substantial."

Mark just stares at his hands on the table. I catch

Raine watching him with that producer's eye that sees everything – the slight tremor in his fingers, the shadows under his eyes, the way he keeps spacing out between responses.

"The routing's brutal this time," she says carefully. Like she used to say to me, when I was pushing too hard. "Even with the changes we made for Lucas."

"I can handle it." Mark's response is automatic. Defensive.

"Sure you can." Chase's voice holds decades of friendship. "Just like you handled that amp explosion. And those missed cues at rehearsal. And—"

"Stop." Mark stands abruptly, chair scraping. "Just... stop."

Lucas catches his arm before he can bolt. "Sit. Eat something. Trust me on this – running doesn't help."

"When did you get so wise?" Mark tries for a smile, but it wobbles.

"When I learned the hard way that being strong sometimes means letting people help." Lucas glances between Raine and me. "Even when you think you can handle everything yourself."

The server arrives before Mark can respond. Devon orders for the table with practiced efficiency – *lawyer mode activated*, Maya calls it. But I notice he gets all of Mark's favorites, remembering details from countless family dinners.

"The vintage guitar collection here is incredible,"

he says once we've all got drinks. Drawing Mark out gently, giving him safer ground. "That early Telecaster in the special exhibit? I've only seen photos."

"'54 model." Mark latches onto the topic like a lifeline. "One of the first with the new headstock design. The original owner—"

He breaks off as his hands shake too hard to lift his water glass. Chase steadies it without comment, the same way he used to steady me when my shoulder was giving out but I wouldn't admit it.

"I can't do this." Mark's voice cracks. "The schedule, the pressure, the constant—" He stops, looks around the table. "Sorry. This is supposed to be about Lucas. About family. Not my... whatever this is."

"This is about family." Raine reaches across the table, covers his trembling hands with hers. "All of us. Even the stubborn ones who think they have to handle everything alone."

Her eyes meet mine as she says it, and I hear everything she's not saying. At least, what I *hope* she's saying, but she looks away too quickly. She still can't hold my gaze.

She still doesn't trust me. Or is it herself she doesn't trust? Either way, I still feel that distance between us. An ever growing chasm that gets wider by the minute.

"Maybe..." Mark stares at his hands under Raine's. "Maybe I need a break. Not right away, or forever. I can finish this leg, I just..."

"Whatever you need. As long as you need." Chase's certainty steadies us all. "The west coast tour can wait. The music can wait. You can't."

"But the routing, the contracts—"

"Are just paper." Devon shifts into lawyer mode. "Easily adjusted. Unlike burning out completely, which has much more serious legal and personal implications."

"Listen to the lawyer," Maya teases gently. "He occasionally knows things."

Our food arrives – Devon ordered enough for a small army. But Mark actually eats, drawn into a discussion about vintage guitars that slowly expands to include Chase's wedding plans, Maya's latest cases, Lucas's new arrangements.

After lunch, we make one last loop through the exhibits. Mark moves slower now, really looking at our history behind glass. At younger versions of ourselves who thought we were invincible. Who didn't know our own limits.

"Hard to believe it's been twenty-five years," he says, stopping at the Hall of Fame display. At the photo of all of us on stage at the induction ceremony, arms around each other, grinning like we'd just booked our first real gig.

"Lot of miles between then and now." Chase studies the photo too. "Good ones and hard ones."

Lucas laughs while pointing at a different display case. "I can't believe you found that old photo from the studio. You know, the one where you're teaching me drums?"

"While your father was recording." Raine's voice is precise. Pointed. "Instead of watching his three-year-old on a drum riser."

"I was right there," I say quietly. "Behind the kit. Where I always was."

"Yes." She meets my eyes for real for the first time. "You were always behind that kit, weren't you?"

The loaded silence that follows feels endless. So, we're back to this part of the rollercoaster. Maya's voice cuts through the tension, too bright: "Is that the gold record display? The one from the first album?"

"Yeah." Chase says quickly. "See the signatures? Your dad insisted we all sign it twice, just in case..."

"Just in case what?" Lucas asks.

"In case we didn't make another one." I remember that day clearly. "In case it was our only shot."

"Always thinking ahead." Raine's tone could freeze water. "About the band, anyway."

"That's not fair." The words slip out before I can stop them.

"No?" She turns to face me fully. "What's not fair,

Will? Pointing out patterns? Noticing how nothing really changes?"

"Mom." Lucas sways slightly, and she's there instantly, supporting him. Maternal instinct overriding everything else.

"You should sit." She guides him to a nearby bench. "Your readings—"

"Are fine." But he lets her fuss, lets her check his monitor. "Just tired."

"Maybe we should head back." Mark suggests carefully. "Get some rest before—"

"Before what?" Raine's sharp tone returns. "The tour you're all so eager to restart?"

"Raine." Chase's warning is gentle but clear.

"No, really." She straightens, and I see the fear rising again beneath her anger. The terror she's turning into blame as our break is coming to an end. "Let's talk about how quickly everyone wants to get back to normal. Back to the schedule that nearly—"

She cuts herself off, but we all hear the unspoken words.

*Nearly killed our son.*

"The schedule's been changed." I keep my voice steady. Calm. "You know that. More rest days, better routing—"

"Better routing." She laughs, but there's no humor in it. "Like Pittsburgh? Having your son in one city while you do press in another?"

"That's not—"

"Lucas needs rest." She cuts me off. "Real rest. Not promises about adjusted schedules or good intentions or—"

"Or what?" The frustration finally breaks through. "Not letting him live his life? Make his own choices?"

"His choices?" Now her voice rises slightly. "Like choosing to skip meals? Push himself too hard? Follow your example?"

"Guys." Lucas tries to stand, but sways again. "Please."

Lucas's obvious exhaustion stops us both cold. In an instant, we're back in that hospital room, watching monitors measure our son's heartbeat. Watching how close we came to losing everything that matters.

"Time to go." Mark's tone leaves no room for argument. "Doctor said not to overdo it."

"Just one more thing." Lucas moves toward the final display – our induction ceremony from last year. The family photo we took on stage, everyone beaming at the camera. "We look so happy."

The words hit hard. That night feels like another lifetime ago now. Before his Cleveland show. Before fear turned to blame turned to this careful distance I don't know how to cross.

"We were," Raine says softly, and I hear everything she's not saying. Everything we're losing.

Maybe everything we've already lost.

Chase moves to help Lucas, but he stumbles slightly. Both Raine and I reach for him instinctively, our hands brushing. For a moment, I feel her trembling. See the fear she's using anger to mask.

She pulls away first.

"Your numbers." Her phone's already out, checking the app that monitors Lucas's glucose levels. Equipment we all have now, a habit born of terror. Her breath catches. "They're dropping again, even though you just ate."

"I'm fine—" Lucas starts, but the slight tremor in his hands betrays him.

"Hotel," Raine says firmly. "Now."

"Mom—"

"She's right." The words cost me, but Lucas's health has to come first. Has to matter more than pride or hurt or whatever's breaking between his mother and me. "You need real rest. And sugar."

"Already on it." Chase has his phone out. "Room service order's going in. The usual?"

"Do you need your glucagon kit?" I ask, worried we might need more drastic measures now than just room service.

"No," Lucas says, shaking his head. And I have to believe him. Have to trust him.

Mark hands Lucas a protein bar from his jacket pocket, and he starts to protest, but another wave of dizziness hits. This time when both Raine and I reach for him, she doesn't pull away. Can't, with our son between us needing both his parents.

"I've got him." My voice comes out rougher than I mean it to.

"*We've* got him," she corrects, but her tone holds more fear than anger now. "Don't we?"

The question feels bigger than this moment. Bigger than just supporting our physically shaky son.

"Always." I meet her eyes over Lucas's head, seeing the tears she's fighting. The terror she's trying to turn into something manageable. Something survivable.

The walk to the exit is slow, measured. Lucas between us, like when he was small. Like when he first got diagnosed and had to learn to navigate the world differently.

"I hate this." His voice is barely a whisper. "Being weak. Being a burden."

"You're not." The words come from both of us. United in this, at least.

"But the tour—"

"Will wait." Raine's tone holds no room for argument. Her eyes stay fixed on her phone, watching his numbers like they might hold some answer to all of this.

"Your mother's right." The admission costs nothing when it comes to Lucas's health. "The music matters. But *you* matter more."

She looks at me then, really looks at me, and I see a flash of something beneath the anger. Understanding. Recognition. The knowledge that some things run deeper than fear or blame or the mistakes we keep making.

But then Lucas sways again, and the moment breaks. We focus on getting him to the car, on making sure he's steady. On being the parents he needs, even if we're barely holding ourselves together.

Even if we're barely holding anything together.

# Gasoline

## RAINE

**THE NEW NETFLIX** deadline won't move. I've known this, have been ignoring the increasingly urgent emails for days, but now it's unavoidable. I have to go back to LA. Have to leave my son while he's still pale, still shaky, still far too close to what almost happened.

Have to trust Will to watch him. The thought sits like ice in my chest.

"I'll be fine." Lucas hugs me at the hotel entrance, and I try not to notice how he leans on the doorframe. How his hands still tremor slightly. "Dad's here, and Mark, and—"

"And you'll check in every three hours." I keep my voice steady. Professional. Like this is just another work trip, not leaving my still-recovering son with the father who... No. Not going there. "No skipping. No matter what."

"Mom." He manages a smile. "The app alerts you automatically. You'll know my numbers before I do."

"That's not the point." But I kiss his forehead, breathing in the scent of him. Alive. Here. Safe, at least for now. "The point is—"

"That you're worried." Will's voice comes from behind me. "We all are. But he's okay. Getting stronger. And you have obligations—"

"Don't." The word comes out sharper than I mean it to. "Just... don't."

Silence falls, heavy with everything we're not saying. Everything we can't say in front of Lucas, who's looking between us with that careful expression he used to wear during the divorce.

"Your car's here." Chase appears with perfect timing, always the buffer. "Want me to grab your bag?"

"I've got it." I hug Lucas one more time, holding maybe too tight. "Three hours. Promise me."

"Promise." He squeezes back. "Love you, Mom."

Will steps forward like he might hug me too, but stops at my expression. "Safe flight."

The careful distance in his voice hurts almost as much as the memory of his arms around me. Of believing things could be different this time. That we could be different.

"Look after him." It comes out like an accusation. Like I don't trust him to do exactly that.

Maybe I don't. Not anymore.

Chase follows me to the car, taking my bag despite my protests. "He'll be okay, you know. Will won't let anything—"

"Like he didn't let anything happen before?" The words taste like fear and blame and all the things I'm trying not to feel.

"Raine." His voice gentles. "You know that's not fair."

"Fair?" I laugh, but there's no humor in it. "Was it fair that our son seized? That his sugar dropped to 32? That Will was in Pittsburgh doing press while Lucas was—"

"While Lucas was making his own choices?" Chase meets my eyes. "Being an adult? Pushing himself too hard, just like his parents taught him to?"

"Don't." I turn away, unable to face the truth in his words. "Just... tell him I'll call when I land."

"Tell him yourself." But Chase hugs me anyway, steady as always. "And Raine? Try to remember you're not the only one terrified of losing him. You can't keep doing this. It's not fair."

The words follow me into the car. Into the airport. Into the first-class seat that feels like running away, like abandoning my son when he needs me most.

My phone buzzes – Lucas's numbers, steady for now. Another buzz – Will, sending the doctor's latest update. A third – Maya asking if I want her to come stay with me for a while.

I turn the phone off, unable to deal with any of it.

Unable to face the reality of leaving, of trusting, of believing anything will be different this time.

The last time I trusted Will with our children's safety, with our future, with my heart...

*No. Not going there either.*

Somewhere over Colorado, I finally turn my phone back on. Three texts from Lucas with his numbers, all steady. One from Maya saying she's packing a bag to stay with me. Two from Netflix about their deadline that can't be pushed anymore.

Nothing from Will.

I close my eyes, but the memories come anyway. Will missing Lucas's first insulin training because of a radio interview. Missing Maya's debate finals for a show. Always for the band, always for the career, always with good intentions that somehow never quite...

My phone buzzes. Lucas's numbers again, slight dip but nothing dangerous. I watch the graph, remembering how his hands shook in that hospital bed. How pale he looked under the fluorescent lights.

How Will wasn't there when it happened.

"Can I get you anything?" The flight attendant's voice breaks through my spiral. "Water? Coffee?"

"I'm fine." But I'm not. Haven't been since that call from Mark. Since hearing my son had seized, had crashed, had nearly...

Another memory surfaces: Will teaching Lucas drums after his diagnosis. Setting up that practice pad in the hospital room. Being there every day of that first recovery, even canceling shows to...

No. I can't think about that. About how steady he can be, how present, how much he loves our children. Can't think about how it felt to trust him again, to believe things could be different this time.

Because nothing's different. He still chose the band first. Still wasn't there when Lucas needed him. Still...

My phone lights up with a photo from Chase – Lucas actually eating lunch, smiling at something off camera. The caption reads: *See? We've got this. All of us.*

All of us. Like we're still a family. Still a unit. Still anything except co-parents trying to navigate another crisis.

The Netflix producers have sent another email. Questions about the final mix, about delivery format, about a thousand details I should be focusing on. But all I can see is Lucas's monitor readout. All I can think about is the miles stretching between us.

Between me and my son.

Between me and the man I thought I could trust again.

A text from Maya pops up.

> MAYA: Mom, stop overthinking everything and call Dad.

I almost laugh. Of course she knows. She's always known us better than we know ourselves.

But I can't call him. Can't hear his voice and stay angry. Can't risk remembering how good we've been, how right it felt to finally stop pretending we didn't still...

The plane hits turbulence, and I grip the armrest. Close my eyes against memories of other bumpy flights, other times Will's voice that got me through rough air. Other times I let myself believe he could be my steady ground.

My phone buzzes one more time. Will, finally.

> WILL: He's asking for your chicken soup recipe. Says the food at the hotel doesn't compare. ☺

Such a simple text. Such a normal moment. Lucas knows damned well I can't really cook. But it breaks something in me, makes me remember all the times Will was there. All the times he did choose us first. All the times I'm trying so hard to forget because remembering hurts too much.

Because remembering means admitting that maybe, just maybe, I'm not just angry at him.

Maybe I'm angry at myself too. For believing. For trusting. For letting him back in only to find out that some patterns really don't change.

*Do they?*

The condo feels wrong when I finally get home.

Too quiet. Too empty. Will's coffee mug still sits by the sink where he left it, before Cleveland, before everything changed. Before I remembered why I stopped trusting him in the first place.

My phone buzzes – Lucas's evening numbers, right where they should be. Another buzz – a photo from Mark showing Lucas actually eating dinner. A third – Maya asking if I made it home safe.

But it's the coffee mug that breaks me. The sight of it there, casual and domestic, like we're still the couple who woke up together all those weeks ago. Still the parents who could handle anything together. Still...

The Netflix deadline looms. I should shower, change, head to the studio. Should focus on work, on obligations, on anything except the memory of Will's face when I wouldn't let him touch me.

I pick up the mug, meaning to wash it. To erase this evidence of what we almost had. What we thought we could have again.

But I can't. Can't erase the memory of morning coffee and sleepy kisses. Can't forget how right it felt to try again, to believe again, to trust...

My phone rings – Lucas.

"Hey, baby." I sink onto the couch, Will's mug still in my hand. "How are you feeling?"

"Better." He sounds stronger, at least. "Dad's being kind of intense about the food thing, though.

Like, I'm pretty sure he's got the hotel kitchen on speed dial."

"Good." The word comes out rougher than I mean it to. "He should be intense about it. After what happened—"

"Mom." His sigh is pure teenager. "I messed up. I know that. But Dad's doing everything right. Maybe too right. He won't even let me look at my kit—"

"Lucas—"

"No, listen." His voice strengthens. "I know you're angry at him. For Pittsburgh, for not being there when... but Mom, he's killing himself trying to make it right. Trying to be what you need him to be."

"What I need?" I laugh, but it comes out wrong. Broken. "I needed him there. When you collapsed. When you seized. When—"

"When I made adult choices that went wrong?" The gentleness in his voice undoes me. "When I pushed too hard, just like you both taught me to?"

"That's not—"

"Fair?" Now he does sound like his father. "Neither is blaming him for my mistakes. For trusting me to handle my own health."

"He promised to watch you."

"And I promised to be careful." He pauses. "We both broke promises, Mom. But only one of us is being punished for it."

The truth of that silences me. Makes me look

again at Will's coffee mug, at all it represents. All we risk losing because I'm too scared to...

"Your father—"

"Loves us." Lucas's voice softens. "All of us. Even when we're making it really hard to."

My phone beeps – the Netflix producers, probably wondering where I am. Wondering why their top vocal producer is running late, missing deadlines, losing focus.

"I have to go." I hate how my voice shakes. "Studio waiting."

"Mom?" He catches me before I hang up. "That song you're producing? The one about second chances?"

"What about it?"

"Maybe listen to the lyrics again." I hear him smile. "Really listen."

I set his father's mug back by the sink. Let my fingers trace its rim, remembering. Hurting. Hoping.

Afraid to hope.

The project awaits. The studio beckons. Professional obligations demand attention.

But all I can think about is a coffee mug, a hospital room, and the man I'm terrified to trust again.

The man I'm more terrified to lose.

Again.

# *Insidious*

### WILL

**ELEVEN PM.** The same time we promised to call every night before the tour. Before Cleveland changed everything. I stare at Raine's contact photo – her laughing in my kitchen, wearing my shirt, hair messy from sleep – and try to convince myself tonight will be different.

It won't be. Hasn't been for two weeks.

Still, I hit dial. Listen to it ring. Wait for her voicemail:

"This is Raine. Leave a message or text details."

Professional. Distant. Nothing like the woman who fell asleep in my arms.

"Hey." My voice echoes in the empty hotel room. "Just checking in. Lucas killed it tonight – stayed steady through the whole set, numbers perfect. He's actually eating the post-show meal for once, if you can believe it. I thought maybe..." I pause, hating how hopeful I sound. How pathetic. "Anyway. Miss you. Both of us do."

I hang up before I can say more. Before I can beg her to talk to me, to let me explain, to understand that I'm trying. That I'm doing everything differently this time.

My phone buzzes – Lucas's glucose readings, automatically sent to all of us. Perfect numbers, just like I said. He's learning. We all are.

Another buzz.

> MAYA: Still no answer?

> ME: No. But her other deadline's tomorrow. Maybe after...

> MAYA: Dad.

I can hear her sigh through the text.

> MAYA: She's not answering because she's scared. You know how she gets.

I do know. God, I do. Know how she retreats when she's terrified. How she uses anger to mask fear. How she pushes away the people she loves most because losing them on her terms hurts less than...

A knock at my door interrupts the thought. Lucas, still in his show clothes.

"You're hovering again." He drops onto my couch,

but I notice he's drinking the protein shake Mark got him. "I can feel you watching my numbers."

"Can you blame me?"

"No." He manages a smile. "But I'm okay, Dad. Really. The new schedule's working, the monitoring system's solid..."

"I know." I sit across from him, trying not to obviously check for signs of fatigue. "You're handling everything right."

"But?"

"But you're my kid." The words come rough. "And just a couple weeks ago you were in the ICU, and I wasn't..."

"Don't." His voice sharpens. "We're not doing that again. I'm an adult who made bad choices. You're a father who trusted me to make better ones."

"Lucas—"

"Mom still not answering?"

The subject change catches me off guard. "She's busy..."

"Right." He rolls his eyes. "Because she can't possibly text during breaks. Or return one of your calls. Or—"

"She's processing." I try for neutral, but probably fail. Try not to let him see how much her silence hurts. "You know how she gets when she's scared."

"Yeah." He stands, stretches carefully. "She pushes away the people she loves most. Especially you."

"It's not—"

"Simple?" His smile is sad now. "No. But it's true. And you know it."

Two more cities, two more unanswered calls. Every night at eleven, like clockwork. Like a promise I can't stop trying to keep, even when she won't let me.

"You're distracted." Chase settles beside me at soundcheck, watching Lucas run through his band's new set across the arena. "He's fine, you know. Numbers are solid."

"I know." But I can't help checking my phone again. Not for Lucas's readings – those are perfect. Have been since we adjusted the schedule, added real breaks, actually made him eat.

No, I'm checking for her.

*Always for her.*

"She'll come around." Chase's voice gentles. "She always does."

"Does she?" I watch Lucas nail a complicated fill, pride mixing with constant worry. "Because last time..."

"Last time was different." He hands me a coffee – the way Raine used to make it. "You were different. The whole situation was different."

"Was it?" The coffee tastes like memory. Like morning kisses and shared showers and everything I thought we were finally getting right. "Because from where she's sitting..."

"From where she's sitting, she's terrified." Mark joins us, his own phone showing Lucas's glucose readings. "And you know how Raine handles terror."

"By running." The words taste bitter. Like coffee gone cold.

"By pushing away what scares her most." Chase corrects. "Namely, you."

"Me?" I laugh, but there's no humor in it. "Pretty sure what scares her most is losing Lucas. Having him crash again because I wasn't—"

"There?" Mark's voice sharpens. "Like you weren't there when he was diagnosed? When he spent a week in the hospital learning his new normal? When he had to relearn drums with shaky hands?"

"That's different—"

"Is it?" Chase takes my coffee, forces me to look at him. "Because I remember you canceling shows. Reworking the entire tour schedule. Putting everything on hold until he was steady."

"Which is exactly what you're doing now," Mark adds. "Even if she can't see it yet."

Across the arena, Lucas finishes his soundcheck. His numbers pop up on my phone – perfect. Steady. Everything we've been working for.

That night after the show, another number pops

up– eleven PM on the west coast. Time for another unanswered call.

"Don't." Chase catches my hand before I can dial. "Not tonight. Give both of you a break."

"We promised." My voice catches. "Every night at eleven. No matter what."

"And you've kept that promise." Mark's tone is gentle. "Every single night. Even when she won't answer. Even when it hurts like hell."

"But maybe," Chase adds, "it's time to let her make the next move. To let her see what she's missing by pushing you away."

"What she's missing?" I watch Lucas pack up his kit, following his post-show routine perfectly. Checking his sugar, drinking his shake, everything we've built into his new normal. "Pretty sure what she's missing is her son."

"No." Chase's voice holds certainty. "What she's missing is seeing you be exactly the father she always needed you to be. The one you are now."

"The one I should have been before."

"The one you were then too." Mark squeezes my shoulder. "Even if neither of you can remember it right now."

My phone sits heavy in my hand as eleven comes and goes. Lucas's numbers are steady after a solid show, the new routine becoming natural. He's thriving under the adjusted schedule, even if he still rolls his eyes at our hovering.

"You're thinking too loud." He appears in my dressing room doorway, protein shake in hand. "About Mom?"

"About a lot of things." I gesture to the couch, trying not to obviously watch how steady he is on his feet now. How strong he's getting. "Mostly about promises."

"The nightly calls?" He settles beside me, close enough that I can smell the venue's fog machine still clinging to his clothes. "Dad, she's not answering. Hasn't answered in weeks."

"I know." The clock ticks further past eleven. "But we promised. Before everything... we promised to stay connected. To do better this time."

"And you are." He sets his empty shake bottle down with deliberate care. "You're doing everything differently. The schedule, the monitoring, the whole setup. But Mom..."

"Is scared." I finish for him. "Of losing you. Of trusting me. Of everything changing again."

"Or maybe of nothing changing." His voice holds a wisdom beyond his years. "Of falling back into old patterns. Old fears."

My phone lights up and goes dark as I play with the screen. So tempted to dial, despite knowing it's futile.

"You know what's funny?" He says softly. "When I was little, after the diagnosis, Mom was the one who pushed too hard. Who hovered and worried and tried to control everything."

"And I was the one telling her to ease up." The memory comes clear. "To let you learn your own limits."

"Exactly." He squeezes my arm. "So maybe now it's your turn to ease up. On her. On the calls. On trying so hard to prove things are different."

"By breaking another promise?"

"By giving her space to miss you." He stands, steady and sure. "To miss us. To remember why she trusted you in the first place."

The clock on my phone stares back at me. Mocking me. My finger hovers over the call button, muscle memory and longing fighting against better judgment.

"Dad." Lucas's voice is gentle. "Let her come back on her own terms. Like you let me find my own way back to the kit. My own balance."

I set the phone down. Let out a breath I feel like I've been holding for weeks.

"When did you get so smart?"

His smile is pure Raine. "Probably around the same time you got so steady. Now get some sleep. We've got interviews tomorrow."

After he leaves, I pick up my phone one more time. Not to call - that urge is finally quiet. Instead, I type a simple text:

ME: Lucas killed it tonight. Numbers perfect. He misses you. So do I. When you're ready... I'm here.

The response comes hours later, just before dawn. Three words that hold more hope than any answered call:

RAINE: I miss you too.

# This Love

### RAINE

I'VE WATCHED his calls come in every night at eleven. Watched that photo I took of him at his kit light up my screen. Watched and couldn't answer, couldn't face hearing his voice, couldn't risk...

But tonight something's different. Eleven comes and goes, and my phone stays dark.

I tell myself this is what I wanted. Space. Distance. Time to process everything that happened in Cleveland. Time to remember why trusting him is dangerous, why letting him in again was a mistake, why...

My fingers find Lucas's monitoring app without conscious thought. His numbers are perfect – have been since they adjusted the tour schedule. Since Will reworked everything to put our son first. Since...

No. I can't think about that. About how steady Will's been, how present, how different from the last time Lucas needed him. How maybe I'm the one who hasn't changed, who's still running, still pushing away, still...

The Netflix tracks are done. Have been for days. I've run out of excuses not to call, not to answer, not to face whatever's left of us after Cleveland broke everything open.

Maya's words from this morning echo in my head: *"Mom, you're punishing him for finally being exactly what you needed him to be thirteen years ago."*

Eleven thirty. Still no call. Again. Second night in a row.

Our simple texts from last night feel like they were sent years ago.

My hands shake slightly as I pull up his contact. The photo I have saved – him teaching Lucas drums after the diagnosis, both of them so focused, so steady, so...

The phone rings three times before he answers.

"Raine?" His voice is rough, surprised. Like he's given up expecting me to call.

Maybe he has.

"I..." The words stick in my throat. All my carefully rehearsed explanations disappear at the sound of his voice. "Lucas's numbers look good."

"Yeah." A pause. "He's doing great. Really found his rhythm with the new schedule."

"The one you arranged." It comes out soft. Breathy. Hesitant. "Putting him first."

"Always." His voice catches. "You know that. Or you used to."

"Will—"

"No, I'm sorry." He takes a breath. "That wasn't fair. You have every right to be angry, to need space, to—"

"Do I?" The question surprises us both. "Have the right to be angry when you're doing everything differently? When you've rearranged the whole tour, when you check his numbers constantly, when you're being exactly what he needs?"

Silence stretches between us, heavy with everything we haven't said. Everything we've been afraid to say.

"Maybe," his voice is careful now, measured, "you have the right to be scared. We both do. After Cleveland..."

"I can't think about Cleveland." My voice catches. "About how close we came to..."

"I know." The understanding in his tone nearly breaks me. "God, Raine, I know. Every time I check his numbers, every time I watch him on stage, I remember..."

"But you're there." The words slip out before I can catch them. "Every show, every reading, every moment. You're exactly where he needs you to be."

"Where I should have been before." He pauses. "Where I'm trying to be now. For both our kids. For..."

The unspoken word hangs between us.

*For you.*

"I saw the tour photos Maya posted." I sink onto my couch, into the spot where he used to sit during morning coffee. "Lucas looks stronger. Happier."

"He is. The new schedule..." He stops. "But you know that. You check his numbers as much as I do."

"Every hour." The admission comes easily. "Sometimes more."

"I know." His laugh is soft, sad. "I see when you log into the app. Used to time my calls around it, hoping..."

"Will." His name catches in my throat.

"It's okay." But his voice says it isn't. Not really. "You needed space. I get it. After everything..."

"Do you?" I curl into myself, missing his warmth beside me. "Get it?"

"You're terrified of trusting me again." The simple truth of it silences me. "Of believing things can be different. That I can be different."

"You are different." The words surprise us both. "That's what scares me most."

"Why?"

"Because..." I close my eyes, remembering how safe I felt in his arms just weeks ago. How right it felt to try again. "Because if you've really changed, if you're really putting family first now, then maybe *I'm* the one still stuck in old patterns. Still running when things get hard. Still pushing away the people I..."

"Love?" His voice is barely a whisper.

"Miss." It's all I can admit right now. All I can handle. "God, Will, I miss you. Both of you. But I'm so scared of..."

"Of what?"

"Of believing in us again." The truth comes out raw, honest. "Of letting myself need you. Of watching you choose the band over family one more time."

"Raine." The pain in his voice matches mine. "Look at Lucas's schedule. At how we've arranged everything. The band isn't first anymore. Hasn't been since Cleveland. Maybe even before that."

"I know." And I do. That's what makes this so hard. "I see it in every decision you make. Every adjustment. Every moment you put him first."

"Put us first." He corrects softly. "All of us."

Silence stretches between us, full of possibility and fear. I find myself touching the empty space beside me on the couch, remembering how it felt to have him here. To believe we could make this work.

"The tour wraps next week," he says finally. "Maya's dress fitting is the day after we get back."

"I know." I've been counting the days, trying not to think about seeing him again. About facing what-ever's left of us after all this. "Lucas says you've been practicing *'At Last.'*"

His laugh is soft, surprised. "He told you about that?"

"Said you keep playing it at soundcheck. That the

band's threatening to hide your sticks if you don't stop."

"Can you blame me?" His voice holds everything we haven't said. "It's our song."

"Will—"

"I know." He stops himself. "Too much, too soon. I just... I miss you, Raine. Miss us. Even when you're angry at me. Even when you're scared. Maybe especially then."

"I'm not angry anymore." The truth of it catches me off guard. "I'm just..."

"Terrified?"

"Yeah." I curl deeper into the couch, wishing he was here. Glad he isn't. "Of wanting this again. Of believing in us again. Of trusting..."

"That I mean it this time?" His voice roughens. "That family really does come first?"

"That I can let myself need you." The admission costs everything. "That I can stop running long enough to see how much you've changed. How much we both have."

"Then stop running." He says it simply, like it's that easy. "Stay still long enough to see me. To really see what's different."

"And if nothing's different?" The old fear creeps in. "If we're just fooling ourselves again?"

"Look at Lucas's schedule." His certainty steadies me. "Look at how we've rebuilt everything around what matters. Around family. Around us."

"Around love?"

"Always around love." He pauses. "Even when you won't answer my calls. Even when you're pushing me away. Even when you're too scared to believe in us."

"I do believe in us." The truth surprises me. "That's what terrifies me most."

His breath catches. "Raine—"

"I have to go." But I don't move. Can't move. "Lucas's numbers—"

"Are perfect." His smile carries through the phone. "You know that. You checked before you called. Don't run away yet."

"Will."

"I know." His voice gentles. "Small steps. But Raine?"

"Yeah?"

"Next time?" The hope in his voice nearly breaks me. "Don't wait so long to call. Please."

I look at his empty coffee mug, still sitting by my sink. At the life we were building before my fear tore us apart again.

"Eleven?" I whisper. "Tomorrow?"

"I'll be here." The promise in those words holds everything. "Always here. Whenever you're ready."

After we hang up, I check Lucas's numbers one more time. Steady. Strong. Protected by a father who finally knows how to put love first.

Maybe it's time I learned how to do the same.

# Last Night On Earth

WILL

**THE LAST HOTEL** room of the tour feels temporary in a way the others haven't. Tomorrow we head home, back to LA, back to real life without the structure of show times and schedules and eleven PM phone calls that have become the highlight of every day.

My phone lights up right on time. She hasn't missed a call in two weeks.

"Hey." Her voice comes warm through the speaker. "How was the show?"

"Good. Solid." I settle onto the hotel couch, where I always take these calls. Where I can pretend she's just in the next room instead of across the country. "Lucas actually ate dinner before playing without needing reminding."

"I saw his numbers." The smile in her voice

makes my chest tight. "He's really got this figured out now."

"Yeah." I watch the city lights through my window, wondering what she's doing right now. If she's curled up on our couch – her couch – in my old shirt like she used to be. "He's grown up a lot this tour."

"We all have." The words come soft, weighted. "Haven't we?"

"Maybe." I close my eyes, remembering how it felt to hold her. To believe we could make this work. "Though some things haven't changed."

"Like what?"

"Like how much I miss you." The admission slips out easily now. These calls have become a space for truth. "How weird it's going to be, being in the same city but not..."

"Together?" She finishes when I trail off.

"Yeah." I run a hand through my hair, grateful she can't see my nervousness. "I got used to this. The calls. The distance making everything simpler somehow."

"Safer," she corrects gently. "Distance makes everything feel safer."

"Until it doesn't." I think about tomorrow's flight. About how close we'll be. About all the ways this fragile peace could shatter. "What happens when we're back? When we have to figure out how to be... whatever we are now?"

Her silence holds understanding. Fear. Hope. Everything we've been slowly rebuilding through these nightly conversations.

"Maya's fitting is Wednesday," Raine says finally. "That's... that's the first time we'll..."

"Yeah." I tap my fingers against my knee, a nervous rhythm. "I've been practicing *'At Last.'*"

Her laugh is soft, surprised. "Lucas mentioned. Said the band's ready to mutiny."

"Can't help it." I smile, remembering how she looked that first time. How young we were, how certain. "Some songs just get under your skin."

"Some people too." Her voice holds something I'm afraid to name. "Will..."

"I know." And I do. Know how fragile this is. How easily we could break everything we've rebuilt. "No pressure. No expectations. Just... being there. For Maya."

"For Maya," she echoes, but we both hear the question underneath. "How's Mark doing?" she asks, obviously changing the subject.

"He's hanging in. Doing better," I say, considering my friend. He really is doing better, but the road is hard on all of us. "Looking forward to the long break coming up. We all are."

"Good. I worry about him too."

"He's thinking about disappearing for a little bit, after the wedding and everything. It'll do him some good, I think."

Silence stretches, comfortable now in a way it wasn't weeks ago. We've learned how to sit with it, how to let it hold all the things we're not ready to say.

"I kept your coffee mug," she says suddenly, out of nowhere. "The one by the sink. From before..."

"Cleveland." The word doesn't hurt as much now. Has become a marker of before and after, of what we lost and what we might find again.

"I wash it sometimes." Her voice goes quiet. "When I miss... when things feel too empty."

"Raine." Her name holds everything I want to say. Everything I'm afraid to say.

"I know." She takes a shaky breath. "Too much. Too soon. But Will?"

"Yeah?"

"I miss more than just phone calls."

The admission hangs between us, too honest to take back, too fragile to push further.

"You know what I miss?" I say finally, giving us both safer ground. "Sunday dinners. Lucas banging pots while Maya does homework at the counter."

"They're not kids anymore." But I hear her smile. "And Lucas still can't cook to save his life, no matter how hard you try to teach him."

"Neither can you." I shift on the couch, wondering if she's remembering the same things I am. All those nights I tried to teach her knife skills, tested my patience in the kitchen. "I always said you were absolutely hopeless."

"*Deliberately* hopeless." Her laugh warms me. "So you'd have to keep teaching me..."

"Oh, is that what happened? Do tell."

"Will." My name holds amusement, affection, warning. "We're supposed to be taking this slow."

"We are." I look at the city lights, imagining tomorrow's flight. Wednesday's fitting. All the moments coming where we'll have to navigate this in person. "Weeks of phone calls slow enough for you?"

"Maybe." She pauses. "But seeing each other..."

"Is going to be different." I finish when she trails off. "Harder. More real."

"More terrifying." Her honesty catches us both off guard. "What if we can't... what if it's not..."

"Like this?" I understand suddenly. These calls have become safe harbor. A way to be close without risking everything. "What if we can't talk like this in person?"

"What if we mess it up again?" Her voice goes quiet. "What if fear makes me run? Makes me push you away? What if—"

"What if we take it one day at a time?" I cut in gently. "One moment at a time? Like we've been doing with Lucas's recovery. With these calls."

"One dress fitting at a time?" I hear her smile return.

"Exactly." I match her tone. "Though fair warning – I might tear up when Maya tries on her dress."

"Might?" Now she laughs outright. "You cried at her kindergarten graduation."

"She was wearing a cap and gown!"

"A paper one."

"Still counts." I smile into the darkness, loving how easy this feels. How right. "Raine?"

"Hmm?"

"I miss everything too."

The silence that follows holds promise. Possibility. Fear and hope and all the things we're slowly learning to say again.

"Call me tomorrow?" she asks finally. "When you land?"

"Always." I pour everything I can't say into that word. Everything we're not ready for yet. "Even if we're in the same city."

"Even then." Her voice softens. "Goodnight, Will."

"Goodnight."

I stay on the couch long after we hang up, watching the city lights blur. Thinking about coffee mugs and Sunday dinners and all the ways love finds its way home.

If you let it.

If you're brave enough to try. To keep fighting.

Only now, I think we both might be fighting for it.

Finally.

# *Landslide*

RAINE

"MOM?" Maya's voice carries from behind the dressing room curtain. "I think... I think this is it. The final version."

My heart catches, remembering her playing dress-up in my closet. Tea parties in my old performance gowns. Now she's getting married, and I'm sitting in an elegant boutique waiting to see my baby in her actual wedding dress.

"Ready when you are, honey."

The curtain pulls back, and suddenly I can't breathe. She's absolutely radiant. The dress is classic but modern – clean lines, subtle beading, a silhouette that makes her look like something out of a dream.

"Maya." My voice catches. "Baby, you're..."

The boutique door chimes softly.

"Sorry I'm late." Will's voice, warm and familiar, fills the space. "Traffic on Wilshire was..."

He trails off as Maya turns, his eyes going wide at the sight of our daughter in her wedding dress. I watch his face cycle through emotions – shock, joy, that particular softness he's always had about our kids.

"Daddy?" Maya's whole face lights up. "You didn't have to..."

"Yes, I did." His voice is rough with emotion. He takes a step forward, then stops, like he's afraid to get too close. To make this too real. "Maya, you look..."

"Don't you dare cry." She points at him, but her own eyes are wet. "Because if you cry, I'll cry, and they just did my makeup for the photos."

"Not crying." But he pulls out a handkerchief – the one he's carried since Lucas was a baby, ever-ready for spills and tears. "Just got something in my eye."

"Both eyes?" I can't help teasing, even as my own throat tightens at the sight of him. At how right it feels to have him here.

He meets my gaze then, and something passes between us. Understanding. Memory. The weight of all our shared moments watching our children grow.

"The alterations are perfect," the seamstress says, breaking our loaded silence. "Just a few final touches..."

Maya steps onto the platform, and Will moves closer, standing near my chair. Close enough that I catch his scent – same cologne he's worn for years, mixed with something that's purely him. Something I've missed more than I want to admit.

"She looks like you," he whispers, just for me. "That same grace. That same light."

"She has your smile." The words come easily, naturally. "Your heart."

His hand brushes mine on the armrest – accident or intention, I'm not sure. But I don't pull away. Can't pull away, not when Maya's beaming at us in the mirror, not when everything feels so perfectly, terrifyingly right.

"The veil next?" The seamstress holds up layers of delicate tulle. "Or should we try the train extended first?"

"Veil," Maya and I say together, making Will laugh softly beside me.

"Like mother, like daughter." His voice holds years of watching us work in studios, finish each other's sentences, share the same instincts. "Though she's smarter than you were about the flowers."

"Hey." I glance at him, fighting a smile. "That jasmine crown was perfect."

"Until it started falling apart during photos." His eyes hold mine, and suddenly I'm twenty-three again, watching him tuck fallen blossoms back into my hair between shots. "Though you still looked beautiful."

"That's my favorite photo," Maya says, adjusting her veil. "The one where you're fixing Mom's flowers and you both forgot the camera was there."

I stand to help with the veil, grateful for the excuse to step away from the heat in Will's eyes, from the memories threatening to overwhelm me.

But as I arrange the delicate tulle, I catch his reflection in the mirror. The way he's watching us both, love plain on his face. The way he still carries his handkerchief, ready for the tears he's barely holding back.

"Perfect." The seamstress steps back, admiring. "Though we might need to adjust the comb slightly..."

"No." Will says, moving closer. "It's exactly right."

"Dad," Maya's eyes meet his in the mirror, teasing. "Lucas says you've been driving the band crazy at rehearsals."

"He's exaggerating." But Will shifts slightly, caught.

"Really?" She grins. "Because he specifically mentioned someone practicing the accompaniment for *'At Last'* over and over..."

"I just want it to be perfect." He glances at me, then away. "When your mother sings at the reception..."

The weight of that song hangs between us. Surprising him with it at our own wedding. Now me singing it at our daughter's reception, with Will playing drums. The symmetry of it all feels almost too perfect, too dangerous.

"Speaking of perfect," Maya says innocently, "I

remember hearing something about a handmade wedding cake disaster?"

"That," I point at her with my free hand while adjusting her veil with the other, "was entirely your father's fault."

"My fault?" Will's eyes dance. "Who tried to add 'just a little more baking powder' at the last minute to make it 'fluffier'?"

"And who said the smoke wasn't that bad?"

"The fire department agreed with me!"

But I can't help smiling, can't help feeling the rightness of having him here. Of sharing these old jokes, these moments, this perfect afternoon with our daughter. Even if the thought of singing that song, with him backing me, makes my heart race in ways I'm not ready to examine.

"We should get a few photos," the seamstress suggests. "For the final fitting record?"

Maya poses while the seamstress snaps several shots, but I'm more aware of Will beside me, of how naturally we've gravitated together on the small boutique sofa. Of how his hand rests next to mine, not quite touching but close enough that I can feel its warmth.

"One with your parents?" The seamstress gestures us up. "A preview of the big day?"

We move to flank Maya, and I'm thrown back to her kindergarten graduation, her high school performances, every moment we've stood like this – a family, despite everything.

"Mom?" Maya's voice brings me back. "You went somewhere just now."

"Just remembering." I smooth an imaginary wrinkle from her dress. "You're still my baby girl who used to parade around in my performance gowns. And now..."

"Now she's getting married." Will's voice is rough. "But she'll always be our baby girl."

"Dad." Maya's eyes fill. "You promised not to make me cry."

"That was before I saw you in the dress." He pulls out that handkerchief again. "All bets are off now."

The seamstress captures the moment – Maya laughing through tears, Will dabbing his eyes, me trying not to join them both. A perfect snapshot of who we are, who we've always been.

"The band's ready, you know." Maya says to me as I help unbutton the back of the dress. "For *'At Last.'* Chase says you've got it down cold."

Will's eyes find mine in the mirror. "Just need to run it with the vocalist."

"We should probably rehearse." The words surprise me as much as him. "Before the reception. Make sure we're..."

"In sync?" His smile holds memory and promise. "Like always?"

"Like always." The agreement comes easier than I expect.

After Maya changes, after final payments and scheduling, we stand awkwardly outside the boutique. None of us quite ready to let go of this perfect afternoon.

"Dinner?" Maya suggests hopefully. "Devon's tied up with client meetings, and Lucas is at rehearsal..."

"I should really..." I start, but the look on her face stops me. On both their faces.

"Just dinner," Will says softly. "The three of us. Like old times."

Like old times. Like new times. Like maybe times still to come.

"Okay." I find myself smiling. "But no more wedding cake stories."

"Deal." His grin is everything I remember. Everything I've missed. "Though the fire department really did say—"

"Will."

His laugh flows over me like a familiar song. Like a rhythm we never really forgot.

Like maybe we're finally ready to dance to it again.

# Give It Up To Love

## WILL

MAYA PICKS OTIUM, because of course she does. Our daughter has always had a gift for subtext, for pushing us toward moments we're trying to avoid. The last time Raine and I were here...

"You're thinking too loud." Maya slides into the booth, deliberately taking the single side so Raine and I have to share. Our families' saying, always on point. "Both of you are."

"Just wondering if the band's forgiven me for all those soundcheck rehearsals," I say smoothly, though from Raine's slight smile, she knows exactly what I'm really thinking about. That kiss in the parking lot here months ago, the one that started everything. Before Cleveland changed it all.

"Chase says you've got the arrangement perfect." Maya grins. "Though I'm not sure it needed quite that many run-throughs."

"I want it to be right." I glance at Raine, remembering how she surprised me with that song at our wedding. How her voice made time stop. "As right as the first time."

"When Mom made you cry in front of all your music friends?" Maya's eyes dance. "There's video evidence, you know."

"Maya Elizabeth." But Raine's tone holds more amusement than warning.

"What? I'm just saying, if we're going to have a nice family dinner, maybe we could stop pretending there isn't an elephant in the room. Or a parking lot. Or whatever."

"How about," Raine cuts in, "we talk about your centerpiece choices? The photos Devon sent were beautiful."

"Smooth deflection, Mom." But she lets us change the subject, launching into details about flowers and place cards and a thousand things I should probably pay more attention to.

Instead, I'm hyperaware of Raine beside me. The careful space between us in the booth. The way she still smells like jasmine and vanilla, like studio coffee, like everything I've missed these past weeks of nightly calls.

"Will?" Her voice startles me. "Maya asked about rehearsal time."

"Sorry." I focus on our daughter, trying to ignore how natural it feels to sit here with them. How right.

"Run it by me again?"

"I just thought maybe you two should practice together before the actual reception." Maya's eyes move between us. "Since it's such a special song for both of you."

"We will." Raine's voice is soft, and I feel her shift slightly closer. "Once we figure out scheduling..."

"And how to be in the same room without..." I trail off, catching myself.

"Without what, Dad?" Maya asks innocently. "Without getting lost in old memories?"

"Without making it awkward," I finish, but Maya's right. Every moment with Raine now is layered with memory. With history. With everything we're trying to navigate.

The waiter arrives with our drinks – Raine's usual whiskey neat, my beer, Maya's wine. Some routines never change, even when everything else has.

"Lucas called earlier," Maya says, shifting topics with practiced ease. "Said the new tour schedule worked perfectly. His numbers have been solid for weeks."

"We know." Raine and I speak together, then share a small smile. Of course we've both been checking the app obsessively.

"Good to know some things never change." Maya takes a sip of wine. "Like you two being completely in sync about us kids."

"Maya." Raine's warning holds affection. "We're just being careful."

"Like you're being careful with each other?"

Before either of us can respond, my phone buzzes. Lucas's readings, right on schedule. I feel Raine lean closer to check – pure instinct, muscle memory from when we used to monitor him together.

"He's good," she says softly, her shoulder brushing mine. "Really good."

"Yeah." I try to focus on the numbers, not on how right she feels beside me. How natural. "The schedule changes made all the difference."

"You made all the difference." Her voice goes quiet, just for me. "Being there. Being steady."

"We both did." I risk meeting her eyes. "All those calls. All those check-ins."

"Even when I wouldn't answer?"

"Especially then."

Maya clears her throat. "You know I can hear you both, right? This intimate moment you're having?"

Raine starts to pull away, but I catch her hand under the table. Just for a moment. Just long enough to feel her fingers squeeze mine before letting go.

"So," I turn back to Maya, ignoring her knowing smile. "Tell me more about these centerpieces."

The evening slips by too quickly. Maya's stories about wedding plans blend into memories, laughter, moments where I almost forget the careful distance we're supposed to be maintaining. Where it feels like any other family dinner, any other night together.

"I should get home." Maya checks her phone. "Devon's probably done with his client meeting by now."

"We'll get the check." Raine reaches for her purse, but I already have my card out.

"Dad." Maya's smile is soft. "Always taking care of us."

"Always will be." I catch Raine's eye, see something shift there. Recognition. Understanding. Maybe even trust.

We walk Maya to her car, standing close in the cool evening air. Close enough that Raine's arm brushes mine, that I can feel her warmth even through my jacket.

"This was nice." Maya hugs us both, lingering a moment. "Like old times. But better maybe?"

"Better?" Raine asks.

"Yeah." She steps back, studying us. "Because you're both actually here. Really here. Not just going through the motions."

The truth of that settles between us as we watch her drive away. As we stand in the same parking lot where everything changed months ago.

"I parked over there." Raine gestures vaguely, but doesn't move.

"I remember." Of course I remember. Remember

everything about that night. That kiss. That moment when possibility felt endless.

"Will—"

"I know." I turn to face her, careful to maintain space between us. "We're taking it slow. Being careful. But Raine?"

"Yeah?"

"Thank you for letting me be here today. For the fitting. For dinner. For..."

"For letting you be our daughter's father?" Her smile holds sadness and understanding. "You never stopped being that. Even when I was angry. Even when I was scared."

"Even when you wouldn't answer my calls?"

"Especially then." She steps closer, then seems to catch herself. "I should go. Early session tomorrow."

"Right." I shove my hands in my pockets to keep from reaching for her. "About rehearsing the song..."

"I'll check my schedule." She takes another step back, but her eyes hold mine. "Maybe next week? After my production deadline?"

"Whenever you're ready." I pour everything I can't say into those words. "I'll be here."

She nods once, then turns toward her car. But at the last moment, she looks back.

"Will?"

"Yeah?"

"I'm glad you came today. That you're..." She

pauses, choosing her words carefully. "That you're still surprising me. After all this time."

I watch her drive away, feeling hope expand in my chest. Remembering how she felt beside me in the restaurant. How right it felt to be together, all three of us.

Like family.

Like maybe, just maybe, we're finding our way back to what matters most.

# Best Times

## RAINE

I'VE NEVER BEEN DOWN in Will's basement studio, and it surprises me. It's both completely new and achingly familiar – state-of-the-art gear mixed with vintage pieces I recognize from our old life. The mic setup that always worked best for my vocals. Small touches that feel like time collapsing.

"You're early." Will's voice carries from behind his kit, and my heart stutters. "I was just coming up to make coffee."

"I brought some." I hold up the carrier from our favorite shop. "Wasn't sure if you'd have a setup down here."

His smile is soft as he takes in the familiar cups. "Just how I like it."

"Of course." I watch him move through the space, so at home here. Taking the coffee with a careful distance between our fingers. "This is... not what I expected."

"No?" He settles back behind his kit – new, but arranged exactly like his old one. "What did you expect?"

"Something more..." I gesture vaguely, taking in the warm wood panels, the comfortable seating area, the small kitchen nook. "Professional? Less..."

"Homey?" He twirls a stick absently. "Maya always says the same thing. Said it feels more like our old place than a proper studio."

"It does." The admission slips out before I can catch it. "Even though it's completely different."

His eyes hold mine for a moment too long. "Some things just feel right, you know? Even in a different space."

"Will." But I'm smiling now, caught between memory and moment. Between then and now.

"I know." He sets the stick down carefully. "Professional. Careful. Just rehearsing."

I wander the space while he sets up, noting the small details. The way he's arranged everything for optimal flow, just like he used to. The acoustic panels that somehow make the room feel cozy instead of sterile. A framed photo of Lucas at his first real session, and another of Maya getting her law degree.

"The band should be here in about an hour." His voice is carefully neutral. "We could run through it once before they arrive. Make sure we've got the timing right."

"Nervous about backing me?" I try for teasing, not sure I nail it.

"Never." The intensity in his voice makes me turn. "Not with you. Never with you."

He's watching me from behind his kit, and suddenly I remember every session we've ever done together. Every time my voice wrapped around his rhythm. Every moment we made magic in studios just like this one.

But not quite like this one. Because this space is purely him – the man he's become, not just the boy I fell in love with. The father who rearranged an entire tour for our son. The musician who's built something beautiful here.

"You've got the charts?" I move toward the mic setup, needing distance from these thoughts.

"On the stand. But Raine?" He waits until I look at him. "We both know you don't need them. Not for this song."

"Will—"

"I know." He holds up his hands. "But you have to admit, it's kind of perfect. You singing this at Maya's wedding, me on drums..."

"Like coming full circle?" My heart clenches at the words.

"Something like that." He adjusts his snare, a

nervous tell I still recognize. "Though this time I promise not to cry in front of everyone."

"You mean like at our wedding?" I smile despite myself. "When I surprised you with it?"

"Exactly like that." His eyes hold mine. "Though maybe this time I'm the one surprising you."

"How?"

Instead of answering, he counts off. The intro is different – softer, more intimate than the big band arrangement I sang at our wedding. Just brushes on cymbals, a gentle pulse that wraps around me like a caress.

Like coming home.

His arrangement binds around my voice like he remembers exactly how I'll phrase each line. Like twenty-five years haven't passed since I first sang this to him. The dynamics rise and fall with my breath, his brushwork so subtle it feels like we're the only two people in the world.

I close my eyes, letting the music take me. Letting myself feel everything I've been trying to ignore. The way we still fit together, the way he still knows exactly how to support my voice, the way...

The final note fades, and the silence that follows feels electric.

"Raine." His voice is rough. When I open my eyes, he's standing, moving toward me with that familiar intensity that always followed our best sessions.

"That was..." I try to find words. Safe words. "The arrangement is beautiful."

"You're beautiful." He stops just short of touching me. "God, Raine, the way you sing that song... it still..."

The studio door opens upstairs. Voices carry down – Chase and Mark arriving early, talking about tempo changes.

Will steps back, running a hand through his shaggy blonde hair. That nervous tell again.

"We should..." He gestures vaguely at his kit.

"Yeah." I smooth my shirt, try to steady my breathing. "The band..."

"Right." But he doesn't move. Keeps looking at me like he did at our wedding. Like he has in every studio we've ever shared. Like maybe...

"There you are!" Chase's voice breaks the moment. "Getting a head start without us?"

"Just running through the arrangement." Will's voice is remarkably steady as he returns to his kit. "Making sure we've got the timing right."

"Right." Chase's knowing look takes in my flushed cheeks, Will's mussed hair. "The timing. That's definitely what you were checking."

Mark elbows him as he sets up his guitar. "Leave them alone. We've got a wedding song to rehearse."

A wedding song. Our song. The one I sang to Will when we were young and certain and forever.

The one we're about to perform for our daughter's first dance with her new husband.

The one that still makes him look at me like that, even after everything.

Maybe especially after everything.

## Open Your Eyes

WILL

CHASE WON'T STOP GRINNING at me as we set up for the full band run-through. He keeps shooting glances between me and Raine, clearly aware of what he and Mark interrupted. What might have happened if they'd been just a few minutes later.

*Had they been on fucking time, instead of early.*

"Tempo felt good in the monitor mix," he says innocently. "What you two were doing before we got here? Nice and... intimate."

I resist the urge to throw a stick at him. "Can we work?"

"Sure." But his smile widens as he tunes his bass. "Though maybe we should give you two another minute to... check the timing again?"

"Chase." Raine's warning carries from the control booth so we can record this, but I hear the smile in her voice. The same one she used to get when the band teased us in studios years ago.

Mark, bless him, focuses on the charts. "The arrangement's different from the wedding version. More stripped down at the start?"

"Yeah." I adjust my monitor mix, trying not to watch Raine through the glass. Trying not to remember how she looked singing just for me moments ago. "Builds slower. Lets her voice..."

"Drive it?" Chase suggests. "Like always?"

Like always. Like every session we've ever done together. Like every time her voice has wrapped around my rhythm, perfect and inevitable and dangerous.

"From the top?" Raine's at the mic now, and her voice in my headphones makes me miss a breath. "Unless you boys need more time to discuss arrangements?"

"Ready when you are." I count off before Chase can make another comment. Before I can think too hard about how right this feels.

The band falls in perfectly – we've been rehearsing this for weeks without her. But something changes the moment Raine starts singing. The dynamics shift, following her phrasing instinctively. Chase and Mark exchange looks as the groove deepens, as everything clicks into place.

As we remember what it's like when she produces

us. When she makes us better than we are without her.

"One more time from the bridge?" Raine's voice in my headphones is pure producer mode now. "Chase, can you pull back on the walkdown?"

"Whatever you say, boss." He adjusts his bass line. "Though I gotta say, this is a hell of a step down from the Hall of Fame induction. Incendiary Ink: from arena rock to wedding band. Maya better appreciate this."

"Hey." Mark grins. "At least we're not doing *'Celebration'* or *'YMCA.'* Yet."

"Don't give the happy couple ideas." I tap my snare rim absently. "Though I did see *'Electric Slide'* on Devon's mother's request list."

"You're kidding." Chase nearly drops his bass. "We are not... I mean, there's a line. We're only doing this one song. We have a reputation to maintain."

"Afraid it'll ruin your rock god image?" Raine's laugh carries through the speakers. "The mighty Chase Avery, forced to play wedding standards?"

"This from the woman who produced three platinum records last year?" He shakes his head. "We've all fallen so far."

"Speak for yourself." Mark adjusts his guitar strap. "I'm counting this as my gift to Maya. Do you know what vintage Les Paul's cost these days?"

"Less than your therapy will if Devon's mom really expects the *'Chicken Dance.'*" Chase shoots me a look. "This is your fault, you know. You and your drummer genes. If Maya had followed you into music instead of law..."

"Then she'd be making us play her gig instead of her wedding." I catch Raine's eye, see her fighting a smile. "Though maybe with better song choices."

"I don't know." Her voice softens. "'*At Last*' worked out pretty well the first time around."

The studio goes quiet. Chase and Mark exchange looks that I carefully ignore.

"From the bridge?" I manage, trying to keep us professional. Trying not to think about the first time she sang this song. About how much every word meant when she sang to me then.

About how much it still does.

"One more full run and we're there." Raine's producer voice is back, but I hear the slight tremor underneath. "Unless the wedding band needs a break?"

"Watch it." Chase twirls his bass cord. "Or we really will add '*Sweet Caroline*' to the setlist."

"You wouldn't dare." But she's laughing now, that real laugh I've missed so much. "Not at our daughter's wedding."

Our daughter. The words hit me hard, make me miss a beat as I count us in. But then her voice wraps around the melody, and everything else falls away. There's just the music, the groove, the perfect way we've always fit together.

"That's the one." She says after, her voice warm in my headphones. "You've got it exactly right, Will."

"Always did." Chase mutters, just loud enough for my monitors to catch.

Mark elbows him as they pack up. "We'll see you guys next week? Final run-through before the big day?"

"Yeah." I start to stand, but Raine's back in the booth, gathering her things. Still here. Still...

"Take your time." Chase's grin is insufferable as he heads for the stairs. "You probably need to... discuss the arrangement more. Make sure you've got all the... dynamics right."

"Get out." But I'm smiling too, can't help it. Even as my heart races watching Raine emerge from the booth.

"They haven't changed." She moves to gather her purse, her notes. Always so careful with her things. With her heart. "Still terrible at subtle."

"Were they trying to be subtle?"

Her laugh is soft. "Fair point."

We end up at the door together, that awkward moment of not knowing how to say goodbye. Not after that performance. That connection. That almost-moment before the band arrived.

"Raine—"

"Will—"

We both stop, share a smile. Like we used to, when we'd try to speak at the same time.

"You first." I manage.

"The arrangement..." She pauses, choosing words carefully. "It's perfect. What you did with it. How you made it..."

"Ours?" The word slips out, but I mean it. "Again?"

Her eyes meet mine, hold. "Yeah. Again."

The silence stretches, full of everything we're not saying. Everything we can't say. Not yet.

"Same time next week?" I ask finally, giving us both safer ground.

"Same time." She steps through the door, but turns back at the last moment. "Will?"

"Yeah?"

"Thank you. For making it beautiful. For making it..." She takes a breath. "For making it mean something. Still."

I watch her climb the stairs, remember how to breathe. Remember we're taking this slow. Remember all the reasons why.

But god, watching her sing our song again...

# Everlong

## RAINE

HIS CAR MOVES past my condo slowly, like it has every night since I moved in. Since long before we started trying again. Since before Cleveland changed everything.

Or maybe showed us what had already changed. And what hasn't.

I watch him from my window, phone in hand, heart racing. Four months ago I would have pretended not to notice. Two months ago I would have been angry about it. Tonight...

Tonight I'm tired of pretending. Of running. Of being scared of how much hasn't changed – and how much has.

I text before I can talk myself out of it.

> ME: I see you. Come in?

His car stops at the corner. For a moment I think he'll drive away, keep to our careful distance. But then he turns around, pulls into my drive.

My hands shake slightly as I open the door. He stands there looking uncertain, hands in his pockets like he used to when we were young.

"Hi." His voice is soft. Careful.

"How long have you been doing the drive-bys?" I ask, stepping back to let him in.

"Since you moved in." No hesitation. No pretense. "Actually...Even when you were with Eric. Even when I thought..."

"When you thought we'd never find our way back here?"

"Yeah." He follows me to the living room but doesn't sit. Like he's not sure of his welcome. "I just... needed to know you were safe."

"I know." I sink onto the couch, gesture for him to join me. "I've always known. Even when I was angry about it. Even when I was pushing you away."

"Raine—"

"Let me finish? Please?" I wait for his nod. "When Lucas collapsed... god, Will, it was like every fear I've ever had came true at once. Every worry about tours and distance and priorities..."

"I know." His voice roughens. "Believe me, I know."

"But that's just it." I turn to face him fully. "You do know. You changed everything – the schedule, the routing, all of it. You became exactly the father I always needed you to be. And that terrified me even more."

"What terrified you?" Will asks softly. "That I changed, or..."

"That maybe I was the one who hadn't." The admission costs me everything, but I don't care. I can't keep doing this to him. To us. "When Lucas was in the hospital, all I could think about was how many times we'd been there before. How many times you'd promised things would be different. And I just... I couldn't see past old fears. Past old patterns."

"So, you pushed me away." There's no accusation in his voice. Just understanding.

"I needed someone to blame." My voice catches. "And blaming you was easier than admitting how scared I was. How scared I still am."

"Of what?"

"Of believing in us again." I look down at my hands, twisting in my lap. "Of trusting that this time really is different. That you really have changed. That we both have."

"But?"

"But watching you these past months..." I meet his eyes, let him see my truth. "The way you've handled everything. The tour changes, the monitoring, the constant check-ins... You're not the same man who missed Maya's debate finals for a show. Who let the band come first."

"No." He shifts closer, careful but certain. "I'm not. Just like you're not the same woman who used to try to control everything. Who couldn't trust anyone else to take care of our kids."

"I let fear make me cruel." The words come easier now. "In Cleveland. After. I said things..."

"You were terrified." His hand finds mine, warm and steady. "We both were. Are."

"But you didn't let fear drive you away." I turn my hand in his, lace our fingers together. "You stayed. You fixed what needed fixing. You became..."

"The man you always needed me to be?"

"The man you always were." I squeeze his fingers. "Under all the pressure and expectations. Under all the patterns we fell into."

Will's thumb traces circles on my palm, a gesture so familiar it makes my throat tight. "You know what I thought about, every night you wouldn't answer my calls?"

"What?"

"That first time Lucas was diagnosed. How you wouldn't sleep. Wouldn't eat. Just sat there watching his monitors until..."

"Until you made me rest." The memory comes clear. "You learned his whole care routine in one night so I could sleep."

"Because that's what we do." His voice goes soft. "Take care of each other. Even when we're scared.

Even when we're angry. Even when we're not together."

"Like checking my condo every night?" I manage a smile. "Even when I was pushing you away?"

"Always." He tugs me closer, until I can rest my head on his shoulder. "Some things don't change, Raine. Even when everything else does."

"I miss you." The words come naturally now. "Not just... this. Us. But working together. Making music together. Being..."

"Partners?" His arms tighten around me. "In everything?"

"Yeah." I breathe him in, let myself feel safe for the first time since Cleveland. "I'm sorry I let fear win. That I couldn't see past old hurts to who we are now."

"And who are we now?"

I pull back enough to see his face. To let him see everything I'm finally ready to say. "Better. Stronger. Ready to do this right."

"This being..."

"Us." I touch his cheek, feel him lean into my hand. "All of it. The good and the scary and the complicated. Together this time."

His smile is everything I remember. Everything I've missed. Everything I want for the rest of our lives.

"Together." He kisses my palm. "Like always."

"Like now." I correct gently. "Not the past. Not what we were. But who we are. Who we've become."

"Partners?" His eyes hold mine, full of love and hope and certainty.

"Partners." I lean in, finally ready to trust. To believe. To love without fear. "In everything."

His kiss tastes like coming home. Like beginning again. Like finally getting it right.

Like love that's worth the wait to understand.

*Thank You*

## WILL

HER KISS TASTES LIKE FORGIVENESS.
Like understanding. Like twenty-five years of loving
her through everything – marriage, divorce, other
relationships, all of it leading us back here. Back
to us.

"Stay." She whispers against my lips. Not a question this time. Not uncertain or afraid.

"You sure?" I pull back enough to see her face, to
really look at her. "We don't have to rush anything."

"Will." Her smile is soft, knowing. "We've been
taking it slow for too long."

"True." I trace her cheek, memorizing this
moment. The way she leans into my touch, the
certainty in her eyes. "But this time I want to get
everything right."

"This is right." She turns to kiss my palm. "We're
right. Finally."

When she stands, holds out her hand, I take it without hesitation. Follow her down the hall to her room – our room now, maybe. The one I've imagined her in during all those nightly drive-bys, all those times I needed to know she was safe.

"I see you, you know." She turns at the doorway. "Every night. Checking on me."

"Old habits." But we both hear the deeper truth. How I've never stopped watching out for her, loving her, needing her.

"New habits too." Her hands find my chest, steady and sure. "Like actually coming inside when I ask. Like being exactly who I need you to be."

"Raine." Her name holds everything I feel. Everything I've always felt.

"I know." She rises on tiptoe to kiss me again, deeper this time. More certain. "I know now."

Time slows, measured in gentle touches and shared breaths. Her hands remember every place that makes me shiver, and mine find all the spots that make her gasp my name. It's familiar and new all at once – the taste of her skin, the way she arches into my touch, the perfect rhythm we've always found together.

"I missed you." She whispers it against my neck as I unbutton her blouse. "Every day. Even when I was angry. Even when I was scared."

"I know." I kiss her collarbone, feel her pulse race. "God, Raine, I know."

Her shirt falls away, and I have to pause. Have to look at her, to really see her. The new silver in her hair catching moonlight, the slight changes time has brought, the essential beauty that's only grown deeper.

"Will." My name holds decades of love.

"You're so beautiful." The words come rough with emotion. "More beautiful now than when we were kids. More everything."

Her laugh vibrates against my chest as she tugs at my shirt. "Smooth talker."

"I keep telling you, I'm a truth teller." I let her pull the fabric away, feel her hands trace familiar paths across my skin. "Always with you."

She finds the scar from my shoulder surgery, the one that almost ended my career. The one she helped me recover from, even after the divorce. Even when we were pretending we could just be friends.

"Remember this?" Her fingers follow the line of healed tissue.

"Remember you being there." I catch her hand, press a kiss to her palm. "Through all of it. The surgery, the rehab..."

"Like you were there for Lucas." She meets my eyes, lets me see everything she's feeling. "Every time. Even when I couldn't see it."

"Always there." I draw her closer, needing her warmth. Her certainty. "Always will be."

Her kiss tastes like promise. Like understanding.

Like love that's weathered every storm and come out stronger.

When we finally come together, it feels inevitable. Like every moment since we met has led us here, to this deeper understanding, this mature love that knows exactly what it wants. What it's worth.

"Stay with me." She breathes against my lips as we move together. Not just for tonight – I hear the deeper meaning. The forever she's asking for.

"Always." My hands find hers, fingers lacing together like they never forgot how. "No more running. No more fear."

"No more pretending." She arches beneath me, perfect and right. "No more hiding what we are."

"Partners." The word holds everything. "In all of it."

Time dissolves into sensation, into the perfect way we fit together, into love that's finally ready to be everything it always could have been. Everything we've grown into being.

After, she curls against me like she used to, head on my chest where she can hear my heartbeat. My fingers trace idle patterns on her skin while moonlight paints silver across the bed.

"You'll have to teach me to cook again." Her voice holds sleepy contentment. "If we're doing this for real."

"Doing what for real?"

"This. Us. Everything." She props up to look at me. "Unless you'd rather keep doing drive-bys every night?"

"Depends." I brush her hair back, loving how she leans into my touch. "Will you let me in like this if I do?"

"Every time." Her smile is everything I've ever wanted. "Though maybe you could just... stay. Skip the driving part."

"You asking me to move in, Sheridan?"

"Maybe." She kisses my chest, right over my heart. "Eventually. When we're ready."

"And when will that be?"

She's quiet for a moment, thoughtful. "When it feels right. Like this does. Like we do."

"No rush." I pull her closer, breathing in the scent of her. Of us. "We've got time."

"All the time we need." She settles against me, warm and real and certain. "To get it right this time."

My phone buzzes on the nightstand – Lucas's nightly glucose reading, steady and strong. Raine reaches over me to check it, that maternal instinct still sharp.

"He's good." I catch her hand, press a kiss to her fingers. "We're all good."

"Better than good." She relaxes back into my arms. "Finally, exactly where we're supposed to be."

I hold her close as her breathing evens out into

sleep. Listen to the quiet of the house – our house, maybe, eventually. When it's right. When we're ready.

For now, there's just this. Us. Together.

# Stand By Me

RAINE

"SO DIFFERENT FROM the dinner at your place." Devon's mother comments as she watches Will help me with my chair. "You two seem... closer now."

She's not wrong. Everything's different since that night he stayed. Since we finally stopped running from what we've always been to each other.

"We are." I smile as Will's hand brushes my shoulder — a casual touch that feels anything but casual. That speaks of certainty and comfort and love we're no longer hiding.

The private dining room at Otium buzzes with pre-wedding energy. Chase and Mark are entertaining Devon's younger cousins with road stories, carefully edited for the audience. Lucas sits between them, monitoring Maya's champagne consumption with the same attention he now gives his own health readings.

"And all these musicians..." Devon's father glances around at the collection of rockstars who've become family. "They're really Maya's uncles?"

"In every way that matters." Will settles beside me, his knee touching mine under the table. "They've been there since she was born. Since before, really."

"Tell them about Maya's first word." Chase calls from down the table. "The one Raine blamed you for."

"Chase." But I'm laughing, remembering. "I don't think—"

"Was it a bad word?" Devon's mother looks scandalized.

"Worse." Will grins. "It was 'cymbal.' She couldn't say 'mama' or 'dada,' but somehow managed 'cymbal' clear as day."

"Because someone," I poke his ribs lightly, "kept letting her bang on his kit instead of practicing actual words."

"Hey, it worked out." He catches my hand, holds it openly on the table. "She turned out perfect."

"She did." Devon's mother watches our linked fingers with understanding. "And now she's getting her happy ending. Like her parents?"

"You should have seen them at the rehearsal last week," Lucas pipes up, grinning. "Mom actually let Dad change the arrangement of *'At Last.'* Without arguing."

"Once." I point my fork at him. "And only because he was right about the tempo."

"Mark it down." Chase raises his glass. "First time in recorded history Raine Sheridan admitted Will Knightly was right about music."

"Not the first time." Will's thumb traces patterns on my hand. "Remember that session at Capitol? When you wanted to speed up the bridge?"

"And you said it needed to breathe?" I lean into him slightly. "Yeah, you were right then too."

"I'm sorry." Devon's father looks between us. "You two work together? Even after..."

"They've always worked together." Maya jumps in. "Mom's the best vocal producer in LA. And Dad's band..."

"Is in the Rock and Roll Hall of Fame." Devon finishes proudly. "Though they're moonlighting as our wedding band tomorrow. Well, for one song, anyway. The important one."

"Speaking of which." Mark sets down his glass. "About that 'Electric Slide' request..."

"Not happening." Chase and Will say together.

"But Mom..." Devon turns to his mother with practiced charm. "What if we got Uncle Chase to do the 'Chicken Dance' instead?"

The look of horror on Chase's face sets the whole table laughing. Even Devon's parents join in, finally relaxing into the strange family their son is marrying into.

"Lucas." Will's voice carries that careful father tone. "Time for numbers?"

Our son pulls out his phone without argument – such a change from months ago. "Steady. Like they have been since..."

He trails off, but we all hear it. Since Cleveland. Since everything changed.

"Good." Will's free hand finds my knee under the table, squeezing gently. Supporting without hovering. "Just checking."

"We all are." Chase's voice holds years of uncle-hood. Of family beyond blood. "Always will be, kid."

"I know." Lucas smiles, that same smile he had at three when the band would let him "play" with them. "Trust me, I know."

As dessert arrives, Devon stands for the traditional thank-you speech. But it's Maya who surprises us all by speaking next.

"I know it's not usual for the bride to make a speech at the rehearsal dinner," she starts, glass in hand. "But nothing about our family has ever been usual."

Will's arm slides around my shoulders, natural and right.

"Tomorrow I'm marrying the love of my life." Maya smiles at Devon. "And I'm so grateful that his wonderful family," she nods to his parents, "is becoming part of our... unique one."

Chase pretends to wipe away a tear while Mark elbows him.

"But what makes tomorrow even more special," she continues, "is seeing my own family whole again. Seeing my parents finally figure out what Lucas and I have known all along – that some love stories are worth waiting for. Worth fighting for. Worth getting right."

"Here, here." Chase raises his glass, and everyone follows suit.

"To family," Devon adds. "Both the ones we're born with and the ones we choose."

"Even if the chosen ones refuse to do the *'Electric Slide,'*" his mother says dryly, and the whole table erupts in laughter.

Later, as the evening winds down, I watch Will with Devon's father, heads bent over a discussion about vintage guitars. Watch Lucas showing Devon's cousins videos from the tour, proud but careful to skip the Cleveland shows. Watch Chase and Mark coordinate tomorrow's schedule with Devon's uncles, professional despite the occasion.

"They're good people." Devon's mother settles beside me. "Your... unconventional family. I see why Maya loves them so much."

"They are." I smile as Will catches my eye across the room, that private smile that's only ever been mine. "They've been there through everything. The good and the hard and the complicated."

"And now?" She glances between Will and me. "Things seem less complicated."

"No." I correct gently. "Just worth it. All of it. The complexity, the history... it's all part of who we are. Who we've become."

Will makes his way back to me, hand automatically finding mine. "Ready to head out? Big day tomorrow."

"The biggest." I lean into him, no longer caring who sees. No longer afraid of showing what we are to each other.

Maya hugs us both goodbye, whispering, "Thank you for getting it right this time."

"We did learn something from you kids." Will kisses her forehead. "About not giving up on what matters."

Outside, the valet brings the car – just one now, since I rode with Will. Since we do most things together these days.

"Stay tonight?" he asks softly as we pull away from the restaurant.

"Don't I always?"

His smile holds everything we've built these past months. Everything we're still building. Everything we finally got right.

"Always," he agrees, and I hear the promise in it. The forever neither of us is afraid of anymore.

# My Little Girl

**MAYA STANDS** before the full-length mirror, and suddenly I'm seeing double – my baby girl in pigtails and princess dresses, overlaid with this radiant woman in white. My hands shake slightly as I adjust my tie, trying to steady myself before I have to speak.

"Daddy?" She turns, and the sight of her stops my breath. "Are you crying already?"

"No." But I'm pulling out my handkerchief – the same one from all her milestones. "Just something in my eye."

"Right." She smooths my lapel, so grown up, so sure. "Like at my kindergarten graduation? And high school? And law school?"

"Those were different." I catch her hand, hold it tight. "You weren't wearing a wedding dress then."

"Will?" Raine appears in the doorway, stunning in

her mother-of-the-bride dress. "The coordinator says ten minutes."

She pauses when she sees us, her eyes going soft. Understanding. I hold out my free hand and she comes to us, completing our circle.

"Look at you." She touches Maya's veil gently. "More beautiful than any dream I ever had for you."

"Mom." Maya's voice wavers. "Don't you start too. My makeup's already going to be ruined from Dad."

"I'm not crying." I protest, but I have to wipe my eyes again. "I just... when did you get so grown up? So ready for this?"

"Probably around the time you and Mom got ready too." She looks between us, at our joined hands, at how naturally we fit together now. "For your second chance."

Raine squeezes my fingers before heading back inside the church, and I draw strength from her touch. From how far we've all come to reach this moment.

The church doors close behind us, giving us one last private moment before the music starts. Maya's hand trembles slightly on my arm, and I cover it with mine.

"Ready?" I ask softly.

"Were you? With Mom?"

The question catches me off guard. "I was terrified. And absolutely certain. Both at once."

"Like I am now?" Her smile is wobbly but real.

"Exactly like that." I kiss her forehead carefully, mindful of her veil. "The best things in life are usually a little scary. Like falling in love. Like letting yourself be happy."

"Like letting your daughter grow up?"

"That's the scariest of all." I manage a smile even as my eyes fill again. "But also the most beautiful."

The music starts – not the traditional wedding march, but a string quartet arrangement of one of my songs. The one I wrote when Maya was born. Because of course that's what she chose.

The doors open, and I catch my first glimpse of what's ahead. Devon standing tall and nervous at the altar. Lucas beaming from his place as best man, looking strong and healthy. The band scattered through the pews, Mark and Chase trying not to cry.

And Raine in the front row, watching us with so much love it takes my breath away.

Maya's hand tightens on my arm as we start down the aisle. Each step feels momentous, weighted with memory. Teaching her to walk. Walking her to her first day of school. Every moment leading to this one, the long walk to her future, where I have to let her go.

Devon's face when he sees her makes my heart catch. It's the same look I still give Raine. The same love that survives everything if you let it.

"I love you, Daddy," Maya whispers as we near the altar.

"I love you too, baby girl." My voice breaks slightly. "Always will."

The minister asks, "Who gives this woman to be married?"

For a moment, I can't speak. Can't let go. Can't do anything except hold my daughter's hand and remember every moment that led us here.

Then Raine catches my eye from the front row, and somehow she knows exactly what I need. Her slight nod steadies me, reminds me that letting go doesn't mean losing. That love only grows when you share it.

"Her mother and I do." My voice comes out clear and strong.

I place Maya's hand in Devon's, and the look they share reminds me of another wedding, another love that felt this certain. When I step back to join Raine, her fingers find mine immediately.

Lucas catches my eye from his place by Devon, gives me that slight nod that means his numbers are good, that everything's okay. That some fears can be conquered with enough love and support.

The ceremony blurs through my tears, but certain moments crystallize with perfect clarity: Maya's voice steady and sure through her vows. Devon's hands shaking slightly as he places the ring on her finger. The way Raine's thumb traces circles on my palm, grounding me through all of it.

When the minister pronounces them husband and

wife, I feel Raine's breath catch. Turn to find her crying too, beautiful and real and mine again. Finally mine, the way we always should have been.

"Ready to perform?" she whispers as Maya and Devon start back down the aisle.

"With you?" I squeeze her hand. "Always."

Maya pauses as she passes us, radiant with joy. Hugs us both together, not separately like she used to have to. Like we're finally the parents she always needed us to be.

"See you at the reception." Her smile holds everything. "Try not to cry during *'At Last.'*"

"No promises." But I'm smiling too, watching our daughter step into her future while holding tight to my own second chance at happiness.

# At Last

RAINE

**THE BAND TAKES** their places behind me as Maya and Devon move to the center of the dance floor. Will catches my eye from behind his kit, and twenty-five years dissolve. I'm singing this song again, but everything's different now. Better. Deeper. More real than when I surprised him with it at our own wedding.

Chase counts us in softly, and Will's brushwork wraps around me just like in rehearsal. Just like always. His arrangement is perfect – intimate and warm, letting the emotion of the song carry through.

Maya leans her head on Devon's shoulder as they begin to dance, and my voice almost catches at the sight. My baby girl, so grown up, so in love, so ready for her own journey. Will's gentle cymbal work steadies me, reminds me to breathe, to feel, to share this moment with everyone.

I close my eyes and let the music take me, feeling every beat Will plays like a caress. Like the love we've finally grown into being. When I open them again, I see tears on Maya's cheeks as she dances, but she's smiling. Devon holds her closer, whispers something that makes her laugh through the tears.

The whole room has gone still, watching. Even the servers have paused, caught in the magic of this moment. Of this song that's meant so much to our family. Mark and Chase play with perfect sensitivity, following every nuance, every breath, but it's Will's drumming I feel in my bones. In my heart.

The music swells, and other couples join Maya and Devon on the floor. Lucas leads Devon's mother out with careful grace, his movements strong and sure. No trace now of the hospital, of fear, of anything except joy in this moment.

I turn slightly, catching Will's eye as I sing. His expression holds everything – pride in our daughter, love for our family, and something deeper, just for me. The same look he gave me when I first sang this song to him. When I surprised him at our wedding with the depth of what I felt.

The arrangement builds exactly as we rehearsed, but it feels different here. More profound. Will's playing wraps around my voice like he's holding me, supporting me, loving me through every note. Mark and Chase follow our lead perfectly, making this more than just a wedding song. Making it our story, Maya's story, everything we've become.

Devon spins Maya gently, and her dress catches the light. For a moment I see her through the years – dancing on Will's feet as a toddler, practicing for her first formal in our living room, and now, moving with such grace in her husband's arms.

The next verse feels like a promise. Not just to Maya and Devon, but to Will. To us. To everything we've finally grown brave enough to be. I don't have to look to know he's crying behind his kit. I can hear it in the delicate way he's playing, in how the music seems to come straight from his heart to mine.

As the song draws to a close, Maya and Devon sway to our music, lost in each other. But then Maya looks up, catches my eye, and mouths "I love you." Her gaze shifts over my shoulder to Will, and her smile grows wider. Happier. Complete in a way it hasn't been since she was small.

The final notes feel like coming home. Will's brushwork fades perfectly with my voice, like we planned it a thousand times instead of just those few rehearsals. Like we've finally learned how to make everything work in harmony – the music, the love, the family we've built.

The room erupts in applause, but I barely hear it. I'm already turning toward Will, drawn by the look in his eyes as he sets his sticks down. He meets me halfway on the side of the platform, pulling me into his arms right there on stage, not caring who sees.

"Perfect," he whispers against my hair. "You're always perfect."

Maya appears beside us, tears streaming freely now. "Mom, Dad... that was..."

"Beautiful," Devon finishes, his arm around her waist. "Though I think you made everyone cry."

"Not everyone." Chase dabs at his eyes. "I just got something in both eyes. At the same time."

"Right." Mark grins. "Must be going around."

Lucas joins us. "That was incredible. Both of you. All of you."

Will's arm tightens around me as we watch our children – our grown, strong, beautiful children – head back to the dance floor. The real wedding band starts up again, something upbeat and joyful, but Will and I stay where we are, wrapped in this moment.

"Dance with me?" he asks softly.

"Always."

We move to the edge of the floor, swaying gently to music we both feel in our souls. Around us, our family celebrates – Maya radiant in Devon's arms, Lucas laughing with his "uncles," love flowing free and perfect.

"Thank you," Will murmurs.

"For what?"

"For singing that song again. For giving us another chance. For making our family whole."

I lean into him, feeling his heartbeat strong and steady against mine. "Thank you for being worth the wait."

The music plays on, and we dance, holding each other close. No more running. No more fear. Just love, finally ready to be everything it was always meant to be.

# *You Make It Real*

## WILL

THE RECEPTION WHIRLS AROUND US, but all I feel is Raine in my arms, her head on my shoulder as we sway to whatever the band is playing. Her voice still echoes in my mind – not just from tonight's performance, but from twenty-five years ago. From every time she's sung our song.

"Maya's about to throw the bouquet," she murmurs against my chest.

"Let her." I pull her closer. "I'm not done dancing with you."

"Will Knightly, professional drummer, refusing to stop dancing?" Her laugh vibrates through me. "What will your rockstar friends say?"

"That I'm exactly where I should be." I press a kiss to her temple. "Where I always should have been."

The crowd cheers as Maya's bouquet flies – probably caught by one of Devon's cousins. Chase takes over the mic to announce the last dance of the night, but Raine and I keep moving to our own rhythm.

"Take me home?" she asks as the final notes fade.

"Your place or mine?"

Her smile holds everything I've ever wanted. "Ours. Eventually. But tonight... I want to dance with you again. Just us."

"We'll need music."

"I think you know the song."

The drive to her condo passes in comfortable silence, her hand in mine the whole way. The day's emotions wrap around us – joy for Maya, pride in Lucas's strength, gratitude for this second chance we've been given.

When we reach her door, I pull her close as she unlocks it. "Dance with me?"

"In the hallway?" But she's already moving into my arms.

"Anywhere. Everywhere. Forever."

Inside her condo – our condo soon, maybe – moonlight spills across the living room floor. Raine kicks off her heels, and I loosen my tie, both of us shedding the formality of the day. When she steps into my arms again, she fits perfectly against me.

I start humming the melody softly, feeling her smile against my chest. Then, barely above a whisper, I sing the opening lines to her. My voice isn't anything special, not like hers, but the words hold every bit of love I've carried all these years.

She joins in, harmonizing instinctively. Her voice joins mine the way it always has in studios, in quiet moments, in every space we've shared. We move together in the moonlight, trading verses, sharing the song that's meant everything to us.

"I like your version," she murmurs between lines. "Even if you're a little flat."

"Hey." I spin her gently. "I'm expressing emotion here."

"Mmm." She settles back against me. "Keep expressing."

We find the harmony again, voices soft in the quiet room. No band backing us now, no crowd watching, no occasion except us. Except love that's finally grown into everything it was meant to be.

Her voice on the bridge makes my heart catch – the same notes she sang at our wedding, at Maya's reception, but different now. Deeper. Richer with understanding and time and the certainty of what we've built.

The last notes fade into comfortable silence, but we keep swaying together. My phone buzzes – Lucas's final reading of the night. Raine checks it without leaving my arms, both of us sharing that parental instinct that never really fades.

"He's good," she says softly. "Everything's good."

"Better than good." I draw her closer, breathing in the familiar scent of her perfume, of us. "Perfect."

"Even if you sing flat?"

"As I said, I was expressing emotion." I kiss her temple. "And you harmonized anyway."

"Always will." She pulls back enough to meet my eyes, and something about her expression makes my heart race. Makes me brave.

"Move in with me." The words come naturally, inevitably. "You're still living out of boxes here anyway."

"Will—"

"I know why you chose this neighborhood." I brush her hair back, loving how she leans into my touch.

"Because it's close to Maya and Devon?" But her smile says she knows better.

"Because it's close to me. To us. To everything we were trying not to want."

She looks around her half-unpacked condo, at the life she's barely started building here. "Your studio is there."

"Our studio." I correct gently. "It always has been. Even before I built it."

"The house is bigger," she admits, biting her bottom lip thoughtfully. "Better kitchen."

"That you still don't know how to use."

"Hey." But she's laughing now, soft and real. "I can make coffee."

"You can make my coffee." I pull her closer again, feeling her heartbeat against mine. "Every morning. In our kitchen."

"In our home?"

"In our everything."

Her smile lights the darkness. "Ask me again."

"Move in with me." I touch my forehead to hers. "Come home."

"Yes." She kisses me gently. "To moving in. To everything. To us."

We start swaying again, humming our song together, harmonizing in the quiet night. No more running, no more fear, no more pretending we're anything except what we've always been.

Partners in everything.

# The Story

"THAT'S THE LAST BOX." Will sets it down in our closet – and it still thrills me to think of it that way. *Our* closet. *Our* room. *Our* home. "Though I'm not sure why you're unpacking these when most of them never got unpacked at the condo."

"I'm nesting." I pull out a stack of sweaters, trying to decide which drawer is now mine. Though really, everything has slowly become ours over the past few months. "It's different this time."

"Because you're actually planning to stay?" His arms slide around my waist from behind, and I lean back into his warmth.

"Because I'm already home."

The house feels different now that it's officially ours. Little touches of me have crept in gradually – my favorite coffee mugs in the kitchen, my throws on the couch. But now, with my condo sold and the last box moved, it feels real.

*Permanent.*

"Maya called earlier." Will nuzzles my neck as I try to organize sweaters. "Said she and Devon are coming for dinner Sunday. Lucas too, if he's not too busy being a rockstar."

"His numbers have been perfect." I can't help checking my phone, that maternal instinct still sharp. "And his band's local tour schedule is working beautifully during the long break before the west coast leg."

"Because his mother is a brilliant producer who knows how to arrange things." He takes the sweaters from my hands, sets them aside. "And because his father finally learned how to put family first."

"We all learned." I turn in his arms, taking in the contentment on his face. The quiet joy that matches mine. "How to balance everything. How to make it all work. God only knows where Mark disappeared to."

"He just needed to get away for a while," he says between kisses down my throat. "Something I definitely *don't* want to do."

His smile is the same one that first made me fall in love with him. The same one that still makes my heart race all these years later.

"Come see something." Will tugs me away from the unpacking, leading me down to the studio. He's been secretive about it all week, saying he was making "adjustments."

The room glows with warm light, and I stop in the doorway, breath catching. He's rearranged everything, creating a perfect blend of both our styles. My favorite mic setup now has pride of place. The vocal booth has been redesigned with the acoustic treatment I prefer. Even the coffee station is stocked with both our favorites.

"When did you do all this?"

"Between sessions." He watches my face carefully. "I wanted it to feel like our space. Not just mine that you're using."

"It's perfect." I move to the console, running my fingers over the board we used to use. The one that's followed us through every iteration of us. "Though I notice my chair is still here. Been saving it for me?"

"Since the day I bought this place." His admission comes quiet, certain. "I think I always knew, somehow. That we'd end up here."

A framed photo catches my eye – new among the collection of family shots on the wall. It's us at Maya's wedding, lost in each other as we danced. The love on both our faces is unmistakable, unguarded.

"Chase took that." Will comes up behind me. "Said he's never seen two people more obviously meant for each other."

"He's not usually right about everything." I lean back against him. "But maybe this time..."

"This time?"

"This time he sees what everyone else apparently

saw all along." I turn to face him. "That we were inevitable. That all roads led here."

"Here being?"

"Home." I kiss him softly. "Together. Finally getting everything right."

Later, we order takeout and eat on the floor of the living room, surrounded by half-unpacked boxes and years of memories. Will keeps stealing glances at me, like he still can't quite believe I'm really here. Really home.

"I have a session tomorrow," I say between bites of pad thai. "Going to feel strange, not driving back to the condo after."

"Good strange?"

"Perfect strange." I steal a piece of his chicken. "Like everything else about us now."

His phone lights up with Lucas's evening reading. We check it together, that parental instinct still sharp but not fearful anymore. Just proud. Grateful.

"Maya texted earlier." Will sets his container aside. "Asked if we're free for brunch next weekend. She and Devon have news."

"If she's pregnant, you're going to cry."

"If she's pregnant, we're all going to cry." He pulls me into his arms, and I go willingly. "Happy tears though. Like at the wedding."

"Like now?" I touch his cheek, feeling the complete rightness of this moment. Of us.

"Always now." He kisses me softly. "Every

morning I wake up with you. Every time I hear you in the studio. Every moment we're finally exactly where we belong."

I look around what used to be just his house, at how naturally our things have mixed together. My books on his shelves, photos on his piano, our life finally, properly merged.

"Play something for me?" I ask, nodding toward the piano.

"At midnight?"

"It's our house now." I settle against him. "We can make music whenever we want."

The song starts soft, gentle, like a heartbeat. Like love that's grown into everything it was meant to be. I hum along, finding the melody that's always been ours.

"I love you," he whispers between notes. "More now than ever."

"I love you too." I close my eyes, completely at peace. "More than any song could say."

# Never Say Never

**THE RING SITS HEAVY** in my pocket as I set up the studio for what Raine thinks is just another session. She's due back from her production meeting any minute, and everything has to be perfect. The band's in position, instruments ready, all of us holding our breath with anticipation.

"You sure about this?" Chase asks quietly, adjusting his bass strap. "The whole band thing?"

"It's us." I check the mic stand one more time. "Music's always been our story."

"Plus," Mark grins, "she can't say no in front of witnesses."

"She won't say no." Lucas speaks up from behind the kit – my old one, the one he learned on. "Mom's been ready for this since before they moved in together."

"Think she suspects?" I fidget with my stick bag,

nervous in a way I haven't been since I was twenty-three and asking her to marry me the first time.

"Dad." Lucas's voice holds affectionate exasperation. "She's been in meetings all day. She has no idea you've got the whole band here to propose with her favorite song."

"Our song," I correct, touching my pocket again. Making sure the ring is still there – the one I had made to match her first one, but different. Like us. Better, stronger, ready for forever this time.

The studio door opens upstairs, and my heart stops. Twenty-five years of loving her, and she still does this to me. Still makes everything else disappear when she walks into a room.

"Will?" Raine's voice carries down the stairs. "Why are the lights...oh."

She stops at the bottom of the stairs, taking in the scene. The full band set up. Lucas at my kit. The mic stand waiting. Her eyes find mine, and I see the moment she realizes this isn't just another session.

"What's going on?"

"We need to cut a track." I move toward her, trying to keep my voice steady. "Something important."

"The whole band? Now?" But she's smiling, that smile that's only ever been mine. "Must be quite a song."

"The most important one." I take her hand, lead her to the mic. "Twenty-five years ago, you surprised me with a song at our wedding. Changed my whole life with those words, that voice, that love."

"Will." Her voice catches as understanding dawns.

"Now it's my turn." I nod to Lucas, who counts us in softly.

The arrangement is different from Maya's wedding version. Stripped down, intimate, just like when we first fell in love. But this time I'm the one singing, my voice carrying all the years of loving her, losing her, finding her again.

She joins in on the second verse, like I knew she would. Like she always has, making everything better. Making us complete. The band follows perfectly, all of us creating this moment together, this foundation for our future.

As the bridge approaches, I step away from the mic. Move to her. Drop to one knee while the music plays on behind us.

"Years ago," I start, my voice rough with emotion, "you surprised me with this song. Made me the happiest man alive. Then life got complicated, and we lost our way. But the music never stopped. The love never died. It just needed time to grow into what it was always meant to be."

Tears stream down her face as I pull out the ring. Behind us, the band plays softly, giving us our moment while still holding the foundation. Like they always have.

"We've done this before," I continue. "But we're

different now. Better. Stronger. Ready to get everything right. So, Raine Sheridan, love of my life, mother of my children, producer of my heart..." My voice catches. "Will you marry me? Again?"

"Yes." She pulls me up, into her arms. "God, Will, yes. Always yes."

The ring slides onto her finger perfectly, catching the studio lights. Different from her first one, but better. Like us.

"Mom?" Lucas's voice carries from behind the kit. "Your mic is still hot."

She laughs through her tears, turning to face our son. "Playing drums at both your parents' proposals. That's got to be some kind of record."

"Actually..." Maya's voice comes through the studio speakers as the control room door opens. "He's not the only one who got to be here this time."

She rushes down to hug us both, Devon right behind her. Even through the tears, I catch the way he protectively steadies her, the subtle roundness of her stomach that reminds me we have more than one thing to celebrate tonight.

"You knew?" Raine asks Maya. "All of you?"

"Who do you think helped Dad design the ring?" Maya grins. "Though Chase wanted him to do it at the Hall of Fame."

"Hey." Chase sets down his bass. "It would have been iconic."

"This is perfect." Raine touches my face, letting

me see everything she's feeling. Everything we've become. "Our studio. Our family. Our song."

"Our future," I whisper against her lips.

The kiss tastes like coming home. Like love that's finally ready for forever.

Like music that never really ended, It just needed time to find its perfect rhythm.

- - THE END - -

# *Force of Will Playlist*

Spotify: https://rebrand.ly/19b200
YouTube: https://rebrand.ly/1178d2

1. *The Sound of Winter*, Bush
2. *Edge of Seventeen,* Stevie Nicks
3. *Ghost of Days Gone By,* Alter Bridge
4. *Going Under,* Evanescence
5. *Your Touch,* Foreign Air
6. *Drumming Song,* Florence + The Machine
7. *So Far Away,* Avenged Sevenfold
8. *23,* The Warning
9. *Through Glass,* Stone Sour
10. *Mud,* Dorothy
11. *DVD,* George Barnett
12. *Silent Stranger,* Against the Current
13. *Breaking Inside,* Shinedown, Lizzy Hale

14. *Everything I Need,* Skylar Grey
15. *Nervous,* Daughtry
16. *Beach Seduction,* The Picturebooks, Leah Wellbaum
17. *Lost In You,* Three Days Grace
18. *Periscope,* Papa Roach, Skylar Grey
19. *Echo,* Trapt
20. *Spell On Me,* Paralandra
21. *Follow You,* Any Given Sin
22. *Choke,* The Warning
23. *Fade In/Fade Out,* Nothing More
24. *Nightmare,* Fame on Fire
25. *Partly Cloudy,* Morgan Page, Skylar Grey
26. *Lioness,* Daughtry
27. *Numb,* Tommee Profitt, Skylar Grey
28. *Dynamite,* Any Given Sin
29. *Show Me The Way You Love,* Leap
30. *Gasoline,* Halsey
31. *Insidious,* Any Given Sin
32. *This Love,* Taylor Swift
33. *Last Night On Earth,* Green Day
34. *Landslide,* Fleetwood Mac
35. *Give It Up To Love,* Somebody's Child
36. *Best Times,* Nothing More, Lacey Sturm
37. *Open Your Eyes,* Alter Bridge
38. *Everlong,* First To Eleven
39. *Thank You,* Led Zeppelin
40. *Stand By Me,* Florence + The Machine

41. *My Little Girl,* Tom Douglas, Tim McGraw
42. *At Last,* Eva Cassidy
43. *You Make It Real,* James Morrison
44. *The Story,* Brandi Carlile
45. *Never Say Never,* The Fray

Thank you

If you enjoyed this book, please consider taking a moment to leave a Review. Even a star rating helps indie authors reach a wider audience.

goodreads       amazon kindle       **BookBub**

*Also by Amy Booker*

## Near Miss RockStar Series

*Almost*

*So Close*

*Barely*

*Near Miss Rock Star Collection*

*In Reach*


## Drive Me Wild Vegas Series

*Ms. Fortune*

*Ms. Chief*

*Ms. Lead*

*Ms. Take*

*The Mischief Motors Collection*


## Rhapsody RockStar Series

*Coda*

*Reprise*

*Overture*

*Waltz*

*Sustain*

# Contact Amy

## FOLLOW

My website: http://www.amybookerauthor.com
Facebook: www.facebook.com/amybookerauthor
Instagram: www.instagram.com/amy_booker_author/
TikTok: www.TikTok.com/@amybookerauthor
Goodreads: www.goodreads.com/author/show/
22225202.Amy_Booker
Amazon: https://rebrand.ly/sraegoj

## BUY DIRECT

Amy Booker Store: https://payhip.com/AmyBooker

## INTERACT

Email: amybookerauthor@gmail.com
Facebook Reader Group: https://www.facebook.com/
groups/amybookersroadies
Newsletter Sign Up: https://www.amybookerauthor.
com/subscribe

## READ EARLY

Join my ARC Team: Find me on Booksprout!